Living with Strangers
STORIES

ELMER HOLMES BOBST AWARD
FOR EMERGING WRITERS

Established in 1983, the Elmer Holmes Bobst Awards in Arts and Letters are presented each year to individuals who have brought true distinction to the American literary scene. Recipients of the Awards include writers as varied as Toni Morrison, John Updike, Russell Baker, Flora Lewis, Edward Albee, Arthur Miller, Joyce Carol Oates, and James Merrill. The Awards were recently expanded to include categories devoted to emerging writers of poetry and fiction, and in 1991 the jurors selected winners in that category, Robert Schirmer for his story collection, *Living with Strangers*, and Laura Kasischke for her collection of poetry, *Wild Brides*.

ROBERT SCHIRMER

Living with Strangers

STORIES

Charlie,
Nice to get to know
you here at Sewanee.

Robert
Schirmer
July '94

NEW YORK UNIVERSITY PRESS
NEW YORK AND LONDON

Library of Congress Cataloging-in-Publication Data

Schirmer, Robert
    Living with strangers / Robert Schirmer.
        p.   cm.
    Includes index.
    ISBN 0-8147-7936-0 — ISBN 8-8147-7937-9 (pbk.)
    I. Title.
PS3569.C499L58   1992
813'.54—dc20   91-28803
                                                           CIP

New York University Press books are printed on acid-free paper,
and their binding materials are chosen for strength and durability.

To my family

CONTENTS

Night Sound   1

The Bats, The Disk   21

Neckers   37

Winter Country   47

Private Room   67

Twilight   89

The Shooting   105

Out of Body   121

Harvest   135

Waiting for the End   161

ACKNOWLEDGMENTS

The author wishes to thank the following magazines in which many of these stories first appeared: *New England Review* ("The Bats, The Disk"), *Indiana Review* ("Harvest"), *Greensboro Review* ("Private Room"), *New Letters* ("Winter Country" under the title "A Place I've Never Been"), *Beloit Fiction Journal* ("Night Sound"), *West Branch* ("Twilight"), *New Mexico Humanities Review* ("Neckers"), and *Descant* ("The Shooting").

ACKNOWLEDGMENTS

Night Sound

At night I wake to someone in my bedroom. It's my brother Cal, standing by the window in a section of moonlight, smoking. He's barefoot, wearing a ratty T-shirt cut off at the chest and a pair of shorts with drawstrings. He says, "Listen, Glen. Sometimes I swear he's outside, calling."

I strain my ears. I listen until my eardrums might pop. What I hear are crickets, mostly. Trains shake the air in town a couple of long miles away. Even as I listen, I know I won't hear anything more because there's nothing more to hear.

"I think I'm asleep," I tell him.

Cal ignores me. What he's listening for, down in the yard and the vegetable garden, is our father, who died two months ago. Since Dad's been dead, Cal works six days a week at a canning factory in town, and comes home smelling like peas. Two nights he also mops and vacuums floors at a Savings and Loan. When he's home, he reads books on karma, spiritual afterlife. What, he wants to know, comes after all this? Some nights he reads hours away, then lights a candle and watches it burn in the living room window. The karma shit makes him hear sounds in the night that aren't there.

"Sometimes I think it's just him I hear," Cal continues. "His boots on the ground." Cal taps cigarette ash into the dirty inside of the window sill, turns to me, sits on my bed. He lowers the cigarette into my mouth and I take a drag. Last month our Aunt Doris drove across two states to check on us. I spent the day shirtless and dirty-toed on the sofa in front of the TV, filling the room with smoke; Cal stared for hours into the candle's blue flame with his legs crossed; Aunt Doris flipped through the occult pages of Cal's guru books and didn't sleep all night. She drove away nervous the next morning, shaking her head, mumbling she'd call. Since then, it's been just Cal and me.

"Don't you ever think about him?" Cal asks, the cigarette back in his mouth.

"Sure," I say. "Sometimes."

"I can't seem to get him out of my head," he says. "I think he's set up camp, right about here." Cal taps his forehead.

He goes on to tell how the air is layered; death simply means passing into the next layer. So even though we can't see or talk to our father, he's still part of the air, we still breathe small pieces of his soul every minute. The Cal sitting on my bed pondering death is not the same loud-mouthed, stringy-haired Cal who, only hours before Dad died, stole Dad's pick-up to go dancing with some girl who works at the town drugstore. That night he asked our father, politely, for the keys to the truck. Dad said "some people" were twenty-one now and didn't need to use the pick-up until they'd found a job and helped pay for gas. Of course, he added, eyebrows raised, the gas issue could be overlooked if these people were willing to admit where they were going and with whom. To this Cal stomped off without a word,

4

nabbed Dad's key chain from the bedroom and went anyway, one-two-threeing the horn as he drove off. There was nothing Dad could do but wait for Cal to come home so he could hit him. He lay on his bed's white sheets, boots still on and tied, fists ready. Later, in my own room, I heard him calling. "Glen!" he yelled once, voice raspy in the night air. I ran to his bedroom, saw him trying to sit up, fingers spread across his chest. A heart vessel gave while we were in the back of the ambulance. One of the ambulance guys said, "Your Pop's just fine, bet on it," then jolted electricity into my father's suddenly still chest. I crawled to a dark cool corner and waited for one of the men to look up and tell me what I already knew.

"I'm sorry," Cal says now, the air over my bed a swirl of his smoke, exhaled breath. When he returned home that night, Cal has told me, usually in the dark so he can't see my reaction—when he came home, he was so stoned he didn't even notice we were gone. He wanted sleep, quiet, darkness. He slept for hours, knowing nothing, until the phone ringing urged him awake.

"I'm sorry," he mumbles again. "I was wrong to come in here and bother you. I just don't want to be alone, you know, when I hear him."

"Maybe just remind yourself he's dead," I say. "Then he can't be in the garden."

Cal's half-smile hangs down. "I'll do that. Thanks. Try to get back to sleep. Sleep is a good thing." He squeezes one side of my neck and chokes me a little, although I know he intends this to be a warm brotherly moment between us.

Because it's late and his guard is down, I ask him if he'll let me ride into town with him in the morning. I could hang out, shoot pool, eat greasy burgers at a bar and grill. Anything but sit around the house all day.

5

Cal shakes his head. "Tomorrow's a bad day, Glen," he whispers. "Maybe soon. Why go into town when you can relax the summer away here? Once your senior years starts up, you'll wish you could stay home, just like you are now."

He stands and I watch him drift back to his room in a trail of cigarette smoke. I know sleep's a long way off for me now. Too much is crowding inside my head. First I think of Cal and me alone in this country house—our father recently dead, mother dead so long who can remember what she looks like? Then I imagine my father, stepping out of air and the sweet corn stalks to call for me. "Glen," he might say, "get out here and water this corn. It's drying out." Or else, "What is it you do off by yourself all day? Come down here and talk to your old man." I try to block my father's voice out, to forget that Cal wants to raise him from the dead. Across the hall I see the candle gleam under Cal's door.

The next night, while Cal's filling the bathtub with steamy water, I walk outside for some space. The first thing I hear is music, coming from the wall of trees that separates our property from the new neighbor's. A few days ago the moving trucks rumbled by, table and chair legs sticking out, and gave me something to look at.

I follow the music past the garden, through the trees, and up behind some shrubs. A girl about my age stands under a floppy basketball hoop hung on a paint-peeling garage wall. In shorts, she stretches while the cassette deck at her feet pounds out The Stones. She leans over one white slender leg, touches a foot, leans over the other leg, touches that foot, arcs her spine back, back, then starts on her toes again. Her ponytail slaps and spins through the air.

6

At her feet lies a half-grown white shepherd dog. It pants, thumps its tail while she swivels, bends. When she's through with the toe touchers, she sits cross-legged on the lawn. She shakes her head free of a rock star head band, then taps her feet impatiently to the music. She gazes into the sky, or maybe across the fields, I can't tell which. I think I hear small sounds coming from her throat, like humming but different, barely carrying in the quiet night. The dog sniffs over and squats on its white haunches. The girl scratches behind its ears. It muzzles her face, then laps salty sweat off her chin and neck. She finger-strokes its spine and the dog's coat shivers. She lowers her tank top a small ways. The dog's tongue dips lower, cleaning the skin over her breasts.

The door of the house opens and out steps a man wearing a white T-shirt. He slices an apple with a small knife. I drop to my knees behind the shrubs. "Sherry," he says.

She pushes the dog away and turns to the man in the doorway.

"What are you doing out here?" he asks.

"I'm stretching, Daddy," she says.

"You're sitting down."

"I decided to take a breather," she says, in a small voice Daddy can't possibly argue with.

The man hacks like a smoker. "Come in pretty soon," he says, clearing his throat. "The mosquitoes are out."

I creep away, back to my house, before her Daddy spots me. Dogs bay like wild things across the fields. Two start up, yelping back and forth, then more join in. Once I saw two dogs trying to mount in our garden, trampling corn stalks, their mouths panting heat. My father charged at them before they got far, waving a whiffle bat over his head. The dogs took off whining.

I grin, remembering this. But how did he know the dogs were there? I didn't see him run from the house or barn, he was just suddenly chasing them.

In the bathroom, Cal's foot dangles over the tub's edge. He looks tired and beat, soaking in water too-hot for a summer bath. He's called me in because he wants to know where I've been.

"Just hanging out," I mumble. I stand quiet, until I'm sure I won't tell him about the girl named Sherry. He doesn't know that her hair is dirty-blonde and her skin salts up when she sweats and her shepherd licks it off while the Stones play. It's a small something that belongs only to me. I say goodnight and go upstairs to my own radio, my secret filling me up, exciting me.

Tonight I don't think about Cal or my father or this house. I think about her, stretching in front of me, bending low for her toes. Then she leans forward, ponytail flipped over one shoulder, and lies beside me on the bed. Downstairs, Cal's voice rises. He might be chanting or he might be talking to himself. I don't listen in.

I go outside the next night, and the next. I hide behind the same mess of shrub and wait for her to show. Soon it's all I look forward to. The days are boring. Cal's off working and I'm alone in the hot house. I sleep until almost noon, then get up for nothing much. I watch TV, read old paperbacks, nap, wait for night. Sometimes I thaw chicken or pork chops for Cal's supper. One day, when I'm feeling both lonely and daring, I go into my father's room. It's stuffy from summer heat but I sit on his bed anyway. A red flannel shirt hangs over one chair, sleeves still rolled. His glasses are tossed open on a pile of business envelopes cluttering his desk. I know I shouldn't be here, that Cal wouldn't like it, but how will he find out? I sit in the room until I'm shivering, then go back to the kitchen and stare out the window toward the woods and Sherry's house. I consider sneaking over, but the sun is shining and the dog is probably nearby. I know I won't feel right, knocking on her door and introducing myself in full light, so I stay put.

Always she's out at night, when the moon lifts into the sky, dogs whoop it up across the fields, and the shadow of Daddy lingers at the window. Sometimes she stretches but sometimes she does other things. She walks down the long driveway, until she and doggie have faded to nothing in the dark. Then, after a minute, they regain shape as they move closer. Sometimes she burns garbage in a metal trash can, sucking in breath as she holds match to paper and fire snaps to life. With a can of bug spray she mists fluttering moths from around the porch light and watches them drop at her feet. One night she swings on the tire hanging from a tree not far from where I hide. Her legs kick air, higher and higher, rope creaking. When she's through she sways in the tire for awhile, fingers drifting up and down her thighs while doggie watches at her feet, muzzle in the dry dirt. Alone, my breath catches in my chest and I want to touch something soft. Instead I bite on my bottom lip. Daddy comes out eventually, calling her name and coughing.

After stretches one night, she starts toward the woods and doggie spots me crouched behind the shrub. It howls once and bounds forward, a white shadow of tooth and jaw snapping out from the dark. I fall back, my face scraping against weeds. One cheek flames up in an itch. I'm so shocked and guilty I don't even try to run. I let the dog leap at me, teeth grabbing my ankle, legs twisting up dirt. "Hey boy," I say while doggie tries to drag me out.

"Sheppie!" the girls says. The dog still tugs so she walks over and swats his butt. Instantly the dog lets go. I rub my ankle.

9

"For Christ's sake," I mumble, just so I'm saying something and not looking guilty.

For a moment she's quiet as she stands over me. "You're trespassing," she says finally. Meanwhile, Sheppie rumbles in his throat. "What are you doing here?" she asks.

"Just watching you stretch." I know it sounds stupid. "I was bored."

I don't know what I expect to say or do, but I don't expect her, after another moment, to nod and sit down cross-legged beside me. "I can only stay for a few minutes," she says. "Daddy's in the house."

Sheppie calls down his guard and romps over to lick my itchy cheek. This helps loosen me up some, but a cigarette would do more. "Do you live over there?" she asks and points to my house, yard light shining through the trees.

"Yeah," I say, offering her a Camel. She shakes her head and says, "No way," so I light one for myself. She watches me, like she can't miss a move.

"You're going to have black lumpy lungs by the time you're twenty," she points out. I shrug and inhale, my heart still kicking.

Mosquitoes dip for her white skin and she fans them away with her hand. "So how many times have you spied on me?" she asks.

"A few times."

She nods and scratches her knees. "What have you seen?" she asks finally.

"I don't know. Not much. Is there something I shouldn't have?"

"How should I know? I don't keep track of every little thing I do."

We sit for a minute and watch my cigarette smoke hang white in the air. I keep one eye on the paint-shredding house for a sign of her father in his sticky T-shirt, knife working the skin off fruit.

"Daddy would kill you, if he knew you were spying," she says.

"Don't tell him then."

"I won't, because he'd kill you. My Mom's in Chicago." She adds this like I asked. "She's waiting until we get settled here, then she's coming out."

I nod. I want to ask her about Chicago, a place I imagine is full of people with things to do, but the house door opens and Daddy steps onto the porch steps. "Sherry!" he calls when he sees she's not under the hoop.

We both hold our breath, then she stands. I notice her feet are bare and broken glass sparkles in the dirt. "Be careful!" I say, meaning don't step on any glass.

"Sssh," she hisses back. "He's just loud. You'll come back, won't you?"

She doesn't really have to ask, it's so obvious.

When I walk into our kitchen a few minutes later, Cal's standing on the table, screwing a light bulb into the ceiling. When he sees me he says, "Glen, your face!" and hops off the table. I remember the weeds then and itch. He hurries me to the bathroom and stands us in front of the mirror. He squeezes a tube of lotion and, behind me, rubs some over the red patch on my cheek. For a moment I notice our reflection in the mirror, him standing so close over me and worried, his breath stirring my hair. I fidget because it makes me uncomfortable, seeing all this under bright lights. In a mirror he looks like our father—his eyes squint and peer, wanting to know everything.

"How did this happen?" he asks. "What have you been into?"
I feel my secret between us. It gleams inside me, down into
the dark of my heart where he can't see. It keeps him from getting too close, even with his breath parting my hair.

"I'm not sure," I say. "I was just sitting around, then I laid
down, and there were some weeds."

He laughs but I see he doesn't believe me. He wants in. "I'll
have to keep my eye on little brother from now on," he says, still
laughing but not really, as I climb the stairs for bed.

I sleep some, then wake, and once more he's in my bedroom, wearing the drawstring shorts and staring into the garden through my window. Only this time, I'm afraid he might
spot Sherry. "Cal," I say. "Come on."

"It's just that I had a dream," he mumbles. "I don't know.
It's so confusing, when you first wake up. Before your head
clears." He moves to the bed and looks down at me. "I don't
want anything to happen to you. That's all."

"Nothing will."

"You're what's left, you and me."

I turn my face into the cool shade of the pillow, away from
his sleepy breath. I can't look at him when he's feeling so low.
"Come on," I repeat. "I know. It's okay."

But later, I dream about my father. He's sitting on the roof
with his shirt open, staring at me from a hole he's punched
through the ceiling. He's wearing his glasses and cleaning his
fingernails with something sharp. The hole brings in so much
light, I need to cover my eyes. I wake sure my father knows
everything—about Sherry, my spying, our whispers in the dark.
The dead can see inside your head, heart, there's no secret place.
I imagine his eyes peering down from the sky, his voice calling,
"Glen!" into the darkness. A small pressure squeezes inside my

temples. Finally I walk to the window and stare out, then up, making sure the sky looks like it always has. The farm dogs keep howling, so lonesome and restless they keep everyone awake.

Soon it's late July and still hot, dry. Twisted corn stalks and bean plants wilt in the fields. Cal puts me in charge of weeding and watering the vegetable garden. He doesn't have the time, he reminds me with watery eyes, and we need to save on grocery bills this winter.

One afternoon when I'm in the garden—shirt off, armpits swampy, back dripping sweat—Sherry steps from the drying woods. She wears an old green house dress. In daylight she looks tall and pale, her eyes shiny but tired too. She's never been to my side of the woods. I feel suddenly nervous.

"Come inside," I whisper. She stares at the house and shakes her head, so I drop the water hose, go to the garden's edge and pull her behind a tree. If Cal came home early, he'd see her and everything would be ruined.

"I wanted to make sure you're okay," she says. "You haven't been over for two nights."

Her hand on my wet arm prickles my skin. I explain that Cal is onto our scent. If we don't skip a few nights, he might find out and then her father would too. Did she want her father to know?

She shrugs. "Who cares?" she says. Then, after a second, "No, of course not." She still holds my arm. We stand for a moment, just like that. "Alright," she says. "As long as I know." She darts back through the woods. I turn around, for a second sure someone is nearby and watching. But I'm alone in my father's garden.

13

The nights we are together, we sit behind the shrubs, listen to the dogs, slap bugs, talk. We talk fast, trying to squeeze everything inside a few minutes. I tell her about my father, how I was alone the night he died, his body convulsing on sheets that sucked the sweat from him. I was alone. The next day, Cal rolled the sheets into the washing machine, dumped in detergent, then tossed the box onto the floor. Tiny blue-white crystals jetted across the tiles. Since, he hasn't been the same.

One night she asks if I miss my father. The question throws me. I can't tell her what I feel, it's all mixed up inside. "I guess," I say. "I think about him a lot."

Sherry admits she misses her mother. If her mother was around, Sherry says, she wouldn't have to play 500 rummy with her father nearly every night. Sherry says they listen to boring ball games on the radio and play until the cards smudge from their greasy fingers. When the cards get too sticky, Daddy tosses the pack into the garbage, whips out another from a kitchen drawer, and they continue playing. Sometimes he'll press his sweaty hand over hers while she's concentrating on how to take a trick. That ruins the game for her. She lets me hold her hand while she tells me this. She knows he just misses her mother, so that's why he's being so close, protective. Once her mother settles matters in Chicago, things will be okay. Until then, she plays cards to keep her father happy. That's why she comes outside, she says. To get away from cards. And that's why Daddy calls her back in. His shuffling fingers are itchy.

And if all that wasn't enough, there's also Sheppie to worry her. She thinks he runs across the fields at night toward the howling. A couple of mornings she's found the fur around his neck speckled with blood. Twice she's caught him chewing on dead rabbits, both half-grown, their bodies limp between his

14

jaws. What if Sheppie doesn't come home one morning and she's left alone with Daddy?

I'm thinking about that when, instead of Daddy, Cal calls from behind the trees. "Glen!" he yells. "Glen?"

I kiss Sherry quick on the cheek and bolt through the woods, coming out in a dark corner of the garden. When Cal sees me, I'm kneeling beside corn stalks, pretending I'm checking how dried up they are. "Don't expect me to believe this picture," he says. I shrug and he shakes his head. "I'm not stupid," he adds. "You're not out here gardening."

Beyond the woods a screen door bangs shut. The light breeze carries the sound right to us. Cal looks toward the trees, squinting. I can hardly breathe, knowing he's getting so close.

"I feel like a walk," I say quickly. "Do you want to come?" Cal pauses but finally takes the bait. We walk across the yard and into a bean field. The beans sag at our feet as we step over them. At first we're quiet, just walking in the open, and I feel pretty good, relaxed. Then a wind smelling like dead crops picks up, blows in our faces and brings out the guru in Cal.

"Wouldn't that be something if we could hear him?" he says, gliding a hand through his wind-stirred hair. "I mean, I know he's here. In the air. But just to see him. Hear him. Wouldn't that be something?"

I stare at the plants I'm stepping over, but all my mind sees is my father shaking in the arms of the ambulance men as they carried him through the kitchen. I see his teeth clamped down in his lips. I shake my thoughts away, but that same pressure's kicked-up inside my temple. Cal wasn't here when our father died. He doesn't stay here all day with no way out.

"Yeah," I mumble. "That would be something."

We walk back in silence. At the house Cal squats under a

tree to chant. I empty dirt from my shoes and go inside for an aspirin. My face in the mirror is white and fearful. I hardly recognize myself.

The next night, while Cal's sweeping up the Savings and Loan, I sneak through the trees and find Sherry tossing cards into a trash can fire. A few cards drift to the ground, others catch and burn in mid-air. When she sees me, she sways forward in a burgundy sundress and sandals. I know something's wrong by the way she's not walking steady. "Here," she says, shoving a small thin bottle at my face. The cap's off and I smell whatever booze she's been drinking.

"Where did you get this?" I ask.

She drops on her knees beside me. "Take some," she whispers.

I manage only a sip, it's so strong. "Great, isn't it?" She leans close. The loose-fitting top of her dress hangs open. I think then how easy it would be to drop my fingers into her dress and touch her small pointed breasts. "I like whiskey," she adds. "I adore whiskey."

"What's wrong?" I rub the back of her neck, nervous at how she leans toward me like a knife pointing, wanting to talk with her face an inch from mine. She's not the same Sherry who stares at the moon and strokes Sheppie into a shiver. Or she is the same, but different too.

Without warning she presses one knee between my legs and kisses me. First I'm so surprised and dumb, I'm not sure what to do. I panic, thinking I'll choke as she glides her tongue around in my mouth and throat. But I quick get the hang of it and kiss back, so dark and deep I taste her sadness mixed in with the whiskey. Something roots in my stomach, legs, and hardens there. I slide my hand under her dress and up the inside of her

16

thighs. While I do this I remember how my father chased dogs from the garden with a bat. But I don't stop. We kiss and press together until we're both out of breath. She pulls away and sits back up.

"I feel sick," she mumbles.

"Sorry."

"It's not you! I mean I'm sick of being here. Sometimes I just want to dump the old man and go away." She tugs on her dress I've mussed, raising a strap back over her shoulder.

"Maybe things will be better once your mother gets here," I say.

Sherry says nothing. Then she shakes her head. "She's not coming," Sherry whispers. "She's staying in Chicago."

"You said she was—"

"She's not coming!" Sherry repeats, louder. She tells me how Daddy talked to her mother on the phone just a few hours ago. When he hung up he drank straight from a bottle, curled up on the living room floor and spread a newspaper over himself. Before he drifted off he talked. "Momma's not coming back," he said. "It's just us now, baby girl."

So I hold her, to get her through this. "It's okay," I whisper, but I think of Cal, the house, the rest of the summer, and I don't believe my own words.

She pulls away, slogs more whiskey, giggles. "Let's run off," she says suddenly. I only stare. "I mean it. To the bend in the road by the field. You know." She stands up, swaying. "Come on. Before Daddy wakes up."

"You can't just leave him on the floor." I say this to stall, because everything is happening too fast.

"Don't be a chicken. It's only for a little bit."

She's looking down at me. I feel an urge kick inside me then. It's like she's passed something through the air and now I want to run too. "If we get caught it's both our asses," I say, standing.

We cut through the woods into my father's garden, dart between the corn stalks, then run across my lawn to the road. The road is dark, a narrow tunnel of gravel leading somewhere we can't see. We run anyway. A slow wind snaps the dried tree branches overhead. Telephone wires and crickets hum above and around us. I run on instinct through the dark, like I'll stop any minute and think better of this. Sherry jogs behind me, yanking on my belt when my pace gets too fast. "Wait," she says, her breath heating the back of my neck. "Slow down."

I sense someone nearby before we reach the bend. When we do, headlights round the curve and shine us down. We scramble into the ditch but the truck squeals to full stop on the road. I know it's Cal before he steps out. Sherry lets out a shrill yelp like a pup. I try to push her farther into the ditch, back into darkness where he won't see her.

"What's going on?" he asks, dangling the keys to the pick-up between his work-calloused fingers. His squint shifts from me to Sherry. "Who are you?" he asks.

She ducks behind me but Cal's still looking. "Stop it!" I say.

"Didn't I ask you what's going on?"

But already his voice quivers. He was returning home for a quiet read and too-hot bath, he wasn't expecting to find me in the ditch with a girl he's never seen. "We wanted to see if we could find our way here in the dark," I mumble. "It's no big deal."

Now Cal eyes me again. We stare each other down. "I'm too tired for this," he says. "If you were thinking about running off, forget it. I have to stop you."

The truck waits on the side of the road for our decision. Cal left the door swinging wide and I hear jazzy music from his tape deck. "Daddy's going to notice I'm gone," Sherry whispers.

Cal hears this and stomps over, big and mad, breath swelling. We back away. His breath whistles out between his teeth.

"Okay, how about we all calm down and take a ride in the truck," he says. "How's that? Then we'll go back and figure out what's happening here."

Sherry and I stay crouched in the ditch, two stalled rabbits ready to run. I can't see Cal's face clearly in the dark. I don't know if he's being straight. Finally Sherry mumbles to herself and walks the few yards to the field. She kicks a few plants, then kneels and stares out.

I walk to her but don't know what to say. Something has ended between us and now starts something else. Who knows what that might be? Cal squats in the ditch to wait and smoke, his trembling fingers gripping the cigarette. I stare over Sherry's shoulder into darkness. I can't see my house.

Then we hear a yell from across the small field. The voice sounds low but clear. "Sherry!" her Daddy calls. She looks up, confused. We listen. "Sherry!" Daddy calls again. "Sherry!"

Cal rises slowly to his feet. I know his skin must be prickling, because I feel goose bumps freckle my own arms. He places one hand across his eyes, like this will help him see better. "Everything's okay!" he calls back, finally, into the night. "Sir? We're on our way."

After this everything is quiet. The fields are quiet, the dogs, Sherry's Daddy. We have no way of knowing if he heard us, though. We stand for another frozen minute, then Cal shivers and walks back to the truck. Sherry and I follow. Cal slides behind the steering wheel while Sherry and I sit in the back of the truck, our legs dangling over the sides but not quite touching.

This time, Cal's as good as his word. Once the truck jerks to a start, he doesn't rush Sherry to her father, but instead drives us home the long way.

The Bats, The Disk

The night Ben almost died he was in the hayloft, watching bats fly from the cracks in the barn ceiling. Their wings sounded in the dusky air like sheets snapping in a hard wind. One moment he was looking up, watching the bats through binoculars, the next moment he backed away, his foot caught in loose twine, and he lost his balance. Too close to the edge, he fell backward from the loft, toward his father's tractor disk he remembered with a sudden clarity was beneath him. In the two brief seconds he fell, his mind filled with an image of the disk—large, hulking, its steel-cold circular blades sharp and still.

He landed slightly forward of the machine, his head resting neatly between two blades. Enough hay covered the floor to cushion his fall, so he only had the wind knocked out of him. The binoculars snapped from his neck and shattered against the disk. Ben lay for several seconds, his back twisted at an angle, trying to breathe, waiting for something more to happen. His ears had plugged up and he couldn't hear the bats.

His father saw all this happen. He was in a far corner of the barn, having just stepped from the stable where the two mangy horses—their only horses—snorted themselves to sleep. He was there for no reason, really, but to smoke, to be alone and stroke the animals' necks. When he heard someone moving out front, he stepped from the stable in time to spot Ben high in the loft, moving toward the edge, staring through his binoculars at the barn's ceiling, sloped and wide like a dome. For a moment he appreciated this sight—his son eager and hopeful, determined to see the world beyond his reach, though he wasn't sure what the boy wanted so badly to see. Then, without warning, a pain stabbed at his chest and he thought, *Be careful, Ben. Don't move too far out.* He was about to say this aloud, but could not, somehow, manage the words.

And then Ben was falling. His father's mouth opened, possibly to scream, and his eyes locked on the disk. He saw clearly how Ben would land, how without sound his back would snap across the blades, and how he would lie there—legs limp, binoculars a noose around his neck, blood running from his mouth. Ben's father dropped to his knees, in the hay and dirt, a scream rising inside but crushed to silence before it reached his throat. He felt the blades within himself, tearing and uprooting. Then Ben landed harmlessly in the hay, his face registering only minor surprise, but still his father could not move. A sound escaped him, finally, a small squeezed sound that quickly turned to dry hacking. He thought he would be sick.

For a few seconds time hung still, off-balance. Ben lay winded in the hay while his father kneeled in the stable's shadows, choking on the one sound that had reached his lips. Then reality shifted gradually into place and his father gained hold of himself. He would not be sick and so, uncertainly, he stood. The barn seemed to him unreal, though, the air heavy and thick, and when he walked forward in small edgy steps, he could not feel his legs or hands or any part of himself. He made his way to Ben anyway, kneeled down, touched the boy's shoulder. "Ben," he said, and then again, in his altered voice, "Ben?"

Ben saw the change in his father's face—the deeper gray of his skin, the mouth now slack in the hard line of jaw, the eyes stunned and gentle as a calf's. "I'm fine," Ben whispered, terrified at what he'd done.

Inside the house, Ben's mother was bent over the bathroom sink, wetting her face with a steamed rag and rubbing Noxzema over her cheeks, forehead, the dark hollows around her eyes. This was her nightly ritual; somewhere she'd read it would shrink her pores and keep her skin smooth to the touch. She was absorbed, staring into the mirror at the thin layer of cream covering her face, anticipating the moment she would wipe the cream away and feel the air against her skin. Then she heard movement at the bathroom door and turned to Ben and her husband. Ben stared down at his shoes while his father squeezed a cap tight in his hands.

"What is it?" she asked them, startled.

Ben's father told the story sparingly. His eyes shifted back and forth, focusing on nothing. "He's lucky he's not dead," the father said. "It's only luck that he's here."

She stood very still, nodding once or twice but feeling numb, like she'd been punched or kicked but could not yet feel the pain. She'd been looking into the mirror, at her face beneath cream, certainly this couldn't have been going on around her. Then she went soft inside, so quickly she had to reach to the sink for

25

balance. Her nerves felt quivering, raw, as though they were resting now on the surface of her skin. If she could have moved at that moment, she would have held them both at once, so close they would have breathed each other's air. She would have done this without thinking twice.

But Ben sensed this swift change in his mother too; he stiffened, drew his shoulders in and backed off, one step. It was nearly imperceptible, this step, but she caught it and understood. So she only asked,

"Honey. Are you all right?"

"I'm fine," he answered.

"You're sure?" She wiped the Noxzema from her face, not noticing the cool rush of air against her cheeks. She washed her hands too. Ben had no visible marks on him, but she did not see this. First she saw him as he would look in a hospital—arms and legs in slings, bandages across his forehead, bruises changing color beneath his clothes. Then she remembered him as a baby, how he'd squirmed in her arms, how when she turned away for a moment and then back again, he would be cramming something into his mouth—clothespins, bottle caps, book ends, Lincoln Logs. There had been no end to his curiosity, it seemed. Once a silver spoon slipped partially down his throat, gagging him. She had run across the room, her heart stalled but her movements confident, and she had reached her fingers inside him, down his throat, and glided the spoon out. He fell asleep on her lap soon after that, exhausted. Remembering this, she washed her hands until the skin was pink and stinging, then reached for a towel and dried each finger individually, still watching Ben in front of her but seeing the small child with a spoon down his throat.

Ben's sister Jolene walked from the kitchen, thumb holding open a slim science fiction paperback. On the cover a woman with wild tumbling hair rode a purple dragon over a mountain smoky with flame. Jolene had to be told—she too was part of the family—so Ben's mother repeated the story hastily, as the father had. Still, Ben's father turned away, unable to listen again. He tossed his crumpled cap onto a chair, then walked to the living room window and lit a cigarette between his lips. When he exhaled, blue smoke exploded from his nose, mouth, throat. Had his father's cigarette smoke always looked blue? Ben wondered, watching the path it curled from mouth to corner to ceiling before disappearing, finally, from sight. And as she spoke, his mother's hands gripping the bath towel—bones tiny and white beneath her skin—had she always been this tense? Ben stared away to avoid seeing Jolene's reaction.

"I'm tired," he said when his mother had finished. "I think I'll go to bed now." Once upstairs, he lay down and picked up his own sci-fi paperback, one about renegade space bacteria that began eating tiny microbes, grew exponentially, and were soon swallowing whole planets, quickly digesting the universe. He didn't feel like reading, though, not tonight. He took off his shirts, jeans, socks and, in his underwear, lay on the bed and stared at the ceiling's yellow stains. The bed was firm, almost hard beneath him. He tried to breath deeply, but his lungs felt hollow. He felt out of place, a stranger in his own room. Ladybird, the family cat, crawled on her belly from behind Ben's desk, fur bristled; Ben stared down, sensing something different about her, then reached over and petted her until the fur was smooth again. Ten minutes after his fall, and he was back in his bedroom with Ladybird, watching the sky fade from blue to black. This seemed odd. Someone knocked on the door but Ben made no move to answer. The knock was Jolene's, he was certain of this, he could see her as if the door was not there—wearing a long white T-shirt as a nightgown, she

27

knocked with her head bowed, listened, considered, tugged at the corner of her mouth, finally slid her knuckles from the door. He knew he should answer, but he did not care to talk about his fall, so he pretended he was already asleep.

And that night he woke once, from a dream in which he was driving a tractor and disk in a large field he could not recognize. The disk blades split the dirt into wide long furrows. Instead of blackbirds or sparrows, the sky was dark with bats, weaving and swooping low. He strained to hear them—their wings—and opened his eyes straining to hear who was pacing the floor beneath his window. He recognized the footsteps as those of his father, normally a heavy sleeper. Ben lay still in the dark, heart thickening with guilt, wondering dimly if his father was barefoot, and if so, how the porch's splintering wood floor felt beneath his toes. Eventually he heard his father walk back inside, close the screen door so it would not creak, and pace the kitchen floor.

At noon, Ben woke to a room white with sun and a shadow at the door. At least he thought it was shadow, at the edge of his sight, but when he turned to look, there was nothing. The ceiling, curtains, bedspread, all shone with a luminosity he could not remember having seen before, though he had also never slept until noon before. He lingered there, swathed in light, until he was more awake and had the energy to call on his body to stand. The shower's water, spit from the weary pipes, prickled at his skin, a mild discomfort. While he scrubbed himself, he remembered his step backward in the hay loft last night. This was a small detail, nudged back to memory from his sleep. He'd wanted only to see the bats more clearly through his binoculars, see them in the night's first flight.

Later, he sat on the tub's edge, warming himself in the window's sunlight and clipping his toenails, made clean and soft from the shower. He took his time going downstairs. The house sounded still, quieted into a dignity beyond the everyday, but he was certain his mother was nearby. The thought of talking about his fall, or even acknowledging it, still unnerved him. When, finally, he stood, a pain prickled between his shoulder and spine, a single red bruise the size of a baby's fist. He rubbed Ben-Gay over the bruise and eyed it a moment longer, as if he expected it to fade and finally disappear.

Downstairs, his mother was sorting laundry into a basket at her feet. When he walked into the living room, she was holding up one of his shirts, as if trying to see through it. Ben felt a familiar stab of guilt, though outwardly he had no reason to feel this way. He had not intentionally fallen. "Ma," he mumbled.

"What?" She was startled, the way his voice pierced her from behind. She tightened her grip on his shirt. She hadn't heard him coming. How could he be so light on his feet, she wondered, particularly when he was wearing boots, as she saw he was? How could she not have known he was coming, *felt* him coming? Since early morning, when the sun first poked through the distant pines, she'd waited for Ben to wake. Actually, her wait had begun even before this, about midway through the long night she'd spent with her husband. He had lain in bed turned away from her, body curled into a bow, trembling slightly beneath the one arm she had slung around him. It was the only comfort she could give that he wouldn't refuse. If they'd been a different couple, maybe she could have held him more firmly and had the courage to ask, in the shadowy night light of the small table lamp, what he had seen out there.

But she could not do this, they were who they were, she could only hold him in that loose everyday way and listen whenever he got up to walk the house and smoke, his slippers softly shuffling across the floor. Somewhere in the long night, she had turned her attention to morning and to seeing Ben again. She wanted to do something special for him, something that would push the fall far from their minds.

So, at first light, she prepared a large breakfast—scrambled eggs, bacon, round fist-sized pancakes, juice—hoping to bring them all together. But the breakfast, too, was a failure. Ben's father, dressed in the same solemn clothes he'd worn yesterday, would not meet her eyes. He picked out one shrivelled strip of bacon from the skillet before he left for work, leaving his cap in the living room where he'd tossed it last night. Jolene came down next, nibbled at a stale piece of toast and gazed around the kitchen with renewed curiosity—the chairs with their uneven legs, the unwashed dishes in the sink, the dried brown leaves fallen from the plant hanging over it. They both sat there for some time, in front of the food, waiting for Ben. A couple of times, an urgency overtook Ben's mother, and she hurried upstairs to check on him, to convince herself he still breathed or twitched or simply slept without complication. Finally, when the breakfast was unsalvageably cold in front of her, she understood he would sleep in today. He was tired, not hungry. So she cleaned off the table, washed the dishes, scrubbed the kitchen white without asking Jolene to do so much as rinse out a sponge. Then she washed clothes, mostly Ben's clothes, still waiting for him to wake.

Now, surprised, pleased, she turned to him, saw in his face his father's eyes—the shyness, the awkwardness around visible emotion. Everything she'd imagined she would say emptied from her head and she felt only confused. "How are you feeling today?" she asked simply and folded the shirt.

"Fine."

"I can fix you something for lunch, if you'd like."

"That's all right," and he shifted his feet. "I'll make a sandwich. I'm not all that hungry."

"A sandwich is probably better. When it's this hot. Jolene made a sandwich."

She handed him the shirt and patted his arm once, briefly. That one touch was all she'd wanted, at first, yet the feel of him—skin light, cool, resistant to her touch—was not what she'd expected. She supposed she should only be grateful that he was alive, and she was grateful, of course she was. But now, at noon, this wasn't quite enough.

Though she could not place what it was she did want.

Ben sensed her disappointment. While eating a bologna sandwich in the kitchen, he wished he'd told her she looked nice. That would have made her happy, or at least feel better, but the moment had passed. He rinsed his plate in the sink, the water sliding between his fingers—a good feeling, he thought. His mother had laid several potatoes on the counter for supper, so he washed these too, loaded them into a metal pot, and went out on the shady back steps to peel them.

Jolene was sitting under a blackening oak, reading her dragon book, and yawning, and thinking of more exciting places, when she saw Ben step from the house. "Hey snoozer!" she was about to yell, then paused. She watched him for awhile, though her eyes were not strong for thirteen and so he appeared somewhat blurry and unfamiliar, standing unmoving at the door, looking toward nothing in particular. She stood up, brushed off her shorts and began walking toward him, surreptitiously, on the balls of her feet, carrying her book and a Coke she'd been drinking, bottle dented at the bottom. Halfway to the house she thought, *I'm sneaking up on him.* She didn't let this realization stop her. She wanted to see what he did when he was alone, was all. Life was so dull sometimes, she thought, except for in books. Ben had brought that kind of mystery and danger into their lives.

So, pressed against the house, she watched as he spread newspaper over the steps, set the pot between his knees, selected a potato, and began peeling. Each of his movements seemed slow to her—deliberate, protracted. The skins dropped soundlessly onto the paper. She heard a bee probing around her head. For two or three minutes she watched him peel, then, dissatisfied, forfeited her cover and stepped out. She wanted to talk to him anyway. Last night she hadn't slept well, kept waking up on edge, breath pointed in her lungs, Ben's name in her mouth.

"You look pale," she said, sitting beside him.

Ben knew what she wanted—she didn't have to say a word—though he couldn't say how he knew this. "I don't want to talk about it," he added.

She raised her eyebrows. "Spooky!" she said and scratched the mosquito bites on her arms. "All I wanted to know was what it was like. It's not a crime to wonder."

Ben stared at the barn and beyond it, to the field of wilted beans. The distant air looked soft in the heat, yet he could see the neighbors' houses very clearly—the roofs, the circle of fences. The road where a car was kicking up a cloud of orange dust.

"Do you remember?" she prodded.

"I fell. What's there to remember?"

"The disk was right under you."

This meant something to Jolene, Ben could see that, but it didn't matter much to him one way or another. "There wasn't time to think about that," he said. This was easier than explaining how it had occurred to him, suddenly and with such force it

32

hadn't been a thought so much as an image, and that he'd been certain he would land on the disk. Except that he hadn't.

"Do you feel different?" Jolene asked. Death experiences changed people, transformed them. She had seen it time and again in her books. She wanted to know this feeling.

"I didn't feel anything. Not really. It just happened." He meant what he said, but at the same time felt he was lying. He peeled the last potato, dropped the knife into the pot and pushed it aside. He also felt tired. His head ached.

"Yeah, I'll bet," she said, folding her arms together, mouth in a frown. *She's so young,* Ben thought, though in years she wasn't that much younger than he. "I can't imagine what it must be like," she added. "To almost die, and then not even get hurt."

Ben thought about the bruise on his shoulder but said nothing.

"Why were you in the hayloft anyway?" she asked, leaning forward to accommodate his secret. "Did you go out to smoke?"

He decided this time to tell the truth. "I wanted to watch the bats come out," he said.

Jolene stared back at him, waiting for more.

At six that evening, when Ben's father still had not returned home, Ben's mother set the table anyway—spaghetti and bread this time, a quick sensible meal that would give the appearance of normalcy, though it was clear to them that all was not normal. They sat down and piled food onto their plates, then stared at it, steam rising into their faces. The silence was very loud.

None of them could know that, a mile away, Ben's father was driving the pickup around the empty country roads, his windows down, the truck filled with the sounds of wind and the hum of locusts, nothing more. He did not turn on the radio. Twice he stopped the truck, stepped out, circled it, stared out over the pasture at his house and barn.

Even driving back there was demanding more energy than he could manage. He did not know how he could face his son or any of them. He'd watched his boy walk to the edge of a high point, had admired this, and when he'd been handed the moment of precognition, he'd been unable to call out and stop the accident. To shout out warning on a hunch or a fear had been beyond him. None of them knew of his peculiar failing, of course, which shamed him more. How could he bear the boy's unknowing glance, his wife's touch, Jolene's voice? The smallest things about them bothered him, now that he was carrying the weight of his secret. So he waited until the sun was dropping low behind the trees, when the sky was no longer so bright and unyielding, before he returned, somewhat reluctantly, to them.

They had finished eating by then. "I'll reheat the spaghetti, it'll take only a quick minute," his wife offered, flying to the stove, grabbing the skillet, but Ben's father shook his head. "I ate two reubens at lunch," he muttered and walked into the bathroom. There he removed his shirt, rolled it into a ball, washed briefly and hard, then picked up the shirt and walked back into the hall, where he felt self-conscious about his bare skin and put the shirt back on. Now they were all in the living room, and he would need to pass them to get to the basement. He saw his son only briefly, from the side . . . the boy's pale face, his thin hands holding another one of those books about dragons and dying planets. *I've lost him*, Ben's father thought, though he could not say how or why. The boy was right there, in front of him. But he barely thought of him as Ben anymore; he kept thinking of him as his son, or the boy, as if Ben's name was slowly being erased from his mind. Shaken, he went downstairs, where it was cool and secret, and Ben's mother, tired from the day's worry and small disappointments, sat in a chair to read a detective novel.

So it was left for Ben and Jolene to return to the barn. Ben needed to do this. He was trying to remember the fall as a full event that would account for everyone's reactions, but all he could recall were individual images and sounds. Twilight slanting through the barn cracks. The smell of aged hay and machinery. The bats' wings flapping. The feel of cold steel as he fell toward the disk. The taste of it in his mouth. This last might have been his imagination. None of it tied together.

He lured Jolene out by promising her a smoke, though she wouldn't go further than the barn door, where it was hazy but not yet dark. They stared at the loft, at old bales spilling wilted straw over the floor, then back at the disk. The spot where he'd landed was still imprinted in the hay, the binoculars still in pieces around the blade. His father had not thought to move the disk from the barn, or even arrange for its removal. Staring at the imprint made Ben mildly curious—he would have liked to walk over, kneel, rest his fingers against it. But he did not do this. Jolene would not understand. So he walked to a shelf in the corner and pulled down an empty, dried-out Texaco motor oil can. He lifted two cigarettes and brought one to her. "Don't drop the match," she instructed him, inhaling. "We don't want to start a fire." So he returned to the shelf and tossed the match inside the can. Overhead, the bats were out in full force, a half dozen at least.

"I hate bats," Jolene said, staring up. "They're so ugly."

"They're all right."

"You really came out to watch bats?"

He shrugged. "Yeah, that's it. I like watching them." They smoked, without much left to say. Except for the bruise on his shoulder Ben was physically the same, yet in a moment his father had grown strange and silent, his mother overly sensitive, Jolene cautious and alert. And inside himself there was a soft emptiness, a cool distance, while everything around him had turned sharp and clear. Twine and one miscalculated step had changed them all, slightly. Again he looked at the disk and again saw it as he had while falling—larger than it was, blades pulling him down, seeking his blood and all that was inside him. He envisioned his body across the blades, split open, spine snapped.

Was this how they saw him now? Was this what divided them? Or had this division been there all along and he was just now seeing it?

Ben did not linger on these thoughts. Instead he focused his complete attention on the bats. He was thinking too much about bats lately. About how they flew. About how their wings were finely tuned radar that helped them avoid, without sight or emotion, the danger they couldn't see but sensed was out there, waiting.

Neckers

Brother waits for those nights when the wind's at the door, sucking at the window screens and whining through the telephone wires above the house. Tonight, when he begins his story, the TV screen in the living room flickers up and down, as if playing his game. From the kitchen, I see only rolling lines and faces.

"Most of them stand or sit in the shadows, like this, doing nothing." He demonstrates in his chair, body soldier-erect and stiff, eyes unfocused. "They don't like light, it shows their faces."

He sits at the kitchen table, chewing on Cornnuts. Between bites he drinks a beer, fingers sliding down the wet bottle. Twenty-one and strong, he works at the Benton State Hospital for the Criminally Insane twelve miles away. Four nights a week, he mops floors, dusts surfaces, empties baskets. On his knees he scrubs the mess out of toilet bowls, sleeves rolled. Whenever Momma suggests he quit his job, her face puckered into small lines, he says, "Someone has to support us," and that shuts Momma up.

"Don't start in on your sister again," Momma pleads now from the screened-in porch, tired of Brother's stories, his tone of voice. The smoke from her cigarette drifts through the open kitchen door. But Brother doesn't listen. He thinks he has control now that he's the only man in the house.

"They don't move a lot," he continues. "They store up energy. Thoughts. Waiting for the right moment." He weighs each word, drawing the mood. "They know more than we think. They're crafty."

We live in the country, the three of us. Two years ago Daddy drove into town for some Lucky Strikes and never came back. The next morning Momma found a letter he'd left in the mailbox. I HAVE TO LEAVE, Daddy wrote. I CAN'T STAY HERE ANYMORE. I'M SORRY. THE CAR'S IN THE LOT BY THE TRAIN STATION. Brother hitched to town and drove the car back. I cried. Momma reread the letter too many times to count and drank cups of coffee. At nights she paced the floor, opened some windows to let in air.

"You're a liar," I say. I feel daring and cocky, talking back to Brother. I'm fourteen and not as quiet as I used to be. "They're not that bad. They're still people."

His eyebrows rise, hang there; he drinks his beer, eyeing me. "Don't be fooled," he says. "They can't be trusted. They don't understand loyalty."

"What about Teddy?" I ask this on purpose, hoping he'll tell me again about big crazy Teddy, who sat for days in the far corner of the hospital TV lounge, watching prime time soaps and smiling. Who Brother befriended, talked with, in the shadows smuggled cigarettes and girlie magazines to. Who one night grabbed Brother's neck and twisted, wanting to snap it like a chicken's. For days Brother carried bruises, shaped like Teddy's thumbs, in the skin around his Adam's apple.

"Listen," Brother says. "I know what I've seen. What do you know, a naive country schoolgirl? They like windy nights. Trees and grass blowing, everything moving. They can hide then. Duck around tree trunks. Slither belly down through the grass like snakes, who's to notice?"

"This is going too far," Momma calls from the porch, but I say, "How can they get in the grass if they're locked up? I thought you said they just sit and think."

"Sit and *wait,*" he says. "For a chance to escape, break free, even for a night. Besides, they only get locked up after they attack. Until then, they're free."

He's always been like this, trying to scare. It's in his blood. When I was little he told me stories that gave me nightmares and woke me up sweating, although even then I wouldn't scream. His stories scared me more than the Friday night horror movies Daddy watched every week, staring, eyes fuzzy like the TV screen that never came in clear, a large bowl of buttered popcorn in his lap. Witches, laboratory freaks, wolf people howling at the moon, psychos who killed with garden tools or kitchen utensils—he watched them all. Vampire movies were his favorite: the thunder, the ancient family curses, the doomed men turning into bats and dropping from the sky, sucking blood from women's veins. Sometimes Brother and I would watch too, me sitting at the foot of Daddy's chair, using his legs as a backrest. If I fell asleep, he carried me to my bed and lay me on top of the covers, never under them. Once, sleepy and confused, I woke up while he carried me and caught him staring down at me, his eyes dark, shiny, and for a second I felt a chill down my back, like I was in a movie. "Daddy," I whispered but he shook his head, set me on my bed without a word.

"This country *breeds* it," Brother continues. "People think the city drives people crazy, but the country does it too—less often, maybe, but worse." The boredom, Brother says, seeps into your brain; you can only take so much flatness and quiet before it fizzes inside your head and motorizes you. You run from it or you do worse. The ones who don't run start roaming the fields and cornstalks at night, mumbling to themselves. Girls hear them down by the lakes, whispering through the milkweeds, making sounds between their teeth like birds trilling. Car headlights catch them darting into the ditch, a flicker of shadow fleeting into shadow.

"Tell Neckers," I say. The time is right—my palms are hot and itch—and it's his best story. He keeps it short, cutting right to Girl and Lover, in the ditch with pants yanked to their knees, thrashing in the grass. A car passes on the road, slows, stops, its beams turned low. "Honey," Girl whispers. "Someone's here." "Ssshhh," he whispers back. "Neckers." She listens, nails pointed into his shoulders, hears nothing, relaxes. Later sneaks away to pee behind a bush and returns to find Lover slashed open like an offering, blood dark, spreading. She runs home through the flat fields, running. Are those footsteps behind her, or the sound of her own pumping heart, panting breath? She climbs a fence and dashes through the yard to her house, screaming, "Daddy, Christ Daddy, help me!" Runs into the dark kitchen where Daddy sits at the table sobbing, sickle still in hand.

When he's finished Brother drinks his beer, knowing "Neckers" gets to me, in small ways, it always has. "Naive pretty girl like you," he adds, staring me down in a way that, for one moment, forces belief. "You better watch out."

42

Momma stomps in, her face flushed. "I said stop it!" She slaps Brother's face, not too hard, then jabs her cigarette butt into the ashtray. He shakes his head and stands up, a red mark on his cheek. "You should be ashamed," Momma says. "Ashamed." She trembles, she's never been the same since Daddy left. She walks me to my room, stands behind me while I undress, strokes my shoulders. Her hand through my hair separates the snarls.

"You shouldn't listen to his stories," Momma says.

"He's just teasing," I answer, feeling bigger than Momma, stronger.

"Don't be scared," she says and I tell her I'm not, I'm not scared. In the kitchen he's moving, looking for food in the cupboards.

I'm not scared, yet I can't sleep that night. Long after Momma's in bed, I listen to the wind through the old boards of the house and think of the men from the state hospital, locked up and dangerous. I imagine their small hard eyes, skin white from no sun, fingers scratching the walls or grabbing Brother's neck. I shiver and know it's time.

I wait until I've worked up the nerve, then sit up and tiptoe barefoot into the hall. Momma's snoring in her room, maybe dreaming about Daddy, how he'll come home one day, slide into bed where she's been waiting, and rest his head between her thighs. From Brother's room there are no sounds. I go onto the porch and peer out the door before stepping into the windy night.

This is part of the game. After Brother tells me his stories, and I'm feeling uneasy, I wait until night and then force myself to walk into the basement without a light, or run down the long driveway and touch the mailbox. I started this when I was eight and he first told me "Neckers," sitting on the edge of my bed in the dark while I lay under the sheets. He whispered so Momma and Daddy, in their bedroom, wouldn't hear. "'Oh Daddy, Lord Daddy, help me!'" he mimicked Girl, his breath in my face smelling like peanuts. That night I only made it across the kitchen, to Daddy's chair on the other side of the table. Tonight I decide I should go as far as the fence at the end of the small field of grass behind the house. My stomach knots, thinking of the distance, but I'm older now. I should go farther and walk, not run.

I take a breath, begin. I hurry around the house, across the lawn and into the field, the long grass brushing my calves. The wind at my back pushes me forward and whistles up my nightie. A distant dog's howl fades to the wind almost before I hear it. Thin clouds like fingers pointing blow across the moon. Everything is alive, stirring, like in a dream or one of Daddy's movies. My heart pounds so swiftly I know how Girl in "Neckers" felt—a heartbeat so hard and physical, it has a rhythm like footsteps. I almost laugh. I can hardly breathe, my chest is so tight. I keep walking anyway. To stop now would be giving into Brother's stories, admitting they're real. If I'm scared, he wins the game.

When I see something move to my right, I stop, my breath stops, heart, everything stops. A second later I realize it's Brother, lying on his back in the bending grass. "Hey," he says, turning to me. "You came out too." I stare down at him, glad I didn't scream or gasp, that I didn't do anything but stop walking.

"Sssh," he adds. "Don't tell Momma." As if she could hear from this distance. "It's such a strange night, I had to come out. To think."

I nod but keep staring, not sure what to do next. I don't finish my dare in front of him. Leaving too quickly would look strange, even though I'm embarrassed that I've caught him lying in the grass so far from the house, shirt off, arms folded under his head. So I don't move.

"Just out for a walk?" he asks. I don't know how much he suspects or knows, so I nod again, hoping he won't ask me any more questions. I could leave then, go back to the house, sneak past Momma's room to my own bed, and forget.

For a moment he's silent, so that the only sound is the wind. Then, quietly, he makes his offer. "Lie down here and take a look," he says, patting the ground beside him. "Take a look at the sky. As long as you're out. Isn't it strange, the way you can feel the wind through the grass?" He holds out his hand to help me down, like I've already said yes, his arm hard and muscled, fingers outstretched, waiting for me. In the moonlight, his eyes shine white.

Winter Country

Winter came early that year. The first storm hurled a foot of snow across the bare fields of southern Minnesota, ripped down telephone lines along the way, and froze some cattle in a small pasture near my home town. An old farmer watching the storm from the kitchen window forgot his cows behind the barn. In the morning, he found them huddled near a fence post, snorting their frozen breath in clouds. Tears frosted their eyes shut. Snow and ice laced their fur in patterns the farmer had not seen before. The legs of one cow had snapped from the cold and the old animal lay apart from the others, licking its bloodied kneecaps. Nearby two calves had died on their sides, half-buried in a swirling drift of snow. My mother said it just went to show the kind of winter we were in for.

One night in the dead center of that winter, my mother called to tell me my stepfather Billy had left her again. When the phone rang, I was reading a newspaper and sitting on the bathtub with my feet in warm water. The radiator in my apartment wasn't working, and my feet don't retain heat. When my girlfriend Sharon had still been living with me, she would often blow on my bare feet and settle them between her thighs. That was during a time in our fading relationship when we weren't comfortable talking to each other, but still felt okay about touching. When that comfort died, too, she packed her things one snowing night while I sat in the kitchen, a respectable distance away, and listened to the soft opening and shutting of the bedroom drawers. Since then, I'd been alone. I tried not to think about that. Done was done.

"Guess who marched out the door with a packed bag?" my mother said. "Just like that, and I'm a swinging single for another night."

"What happened this time?"

"The usual. He called me names. He said I had no soul. Then he broke his favorite coffeecup in the sink. You know, the one with the big red B on the front." She sounded high. Her voice had that edge.

"I don't know why you keep putting up with him," I told her. "Maybe you should take off yourself this time. I'll come get you."

"Stop it. I'm worried. He forgot his gloves and it's so cold."

"You know he'll come back," I said. "He always does."

I drove out of the city and to her house anyway. She told me that wasn't necessary, but what else was I doing? The apartment was cold, my feet wouldn't circulate, nothing was on TV but news and Carson reruns. When my mother smoked pot she got depressed, and my mother depressed was not something I could bear for long.

I stopped at a video store on my way but didn't immediately go inside. Instead, I sat in the car to smoke a quick cigarette and stare out past the slick iced-over fields. I could think more clearly away from my apartment and the deafening silences that my stereo couldn't begin to fill. And what I thought about was Billy, somewhere in the darkness beyond my windshield, drinking in a bar or watching TV in a small but clean motel room while my mother worried at home and sucked on pot. I had no special liking for my stepfather, though Billy had been around for most of my childhood and I barely remembered my real father. If my mother had asked me, I would have advised her to leave Billy and their isolated country house a long time ago. Someday she'd be an old woman, after all, with white hair and weak legs, and wouldn't be able to get out in a hurry, even if she needed to.

When I walked into the house my mother was lying on the living room carpet with her stockinged feet propped on the sofa. She held a joint in one hand and Billy's leather gloves in the other. "Stomp your feet," she said. "I feel simply and absolutely awful, you know, you driving all this way to babysit me."

I stepped out of my boots, peeled off a layer of socks, and lay down beside her. Her hair smelled like herbal shampoo. "If I can freeload a few hits off you, we'll call it square," I told her.

So we passed the joint back and forth. "I don't like to think of him driving without gloves," she said. "The steering wheel gets so cold." She reminded me how sensitive Billy's hand was. He'd broken it many years ago and it had never healed quite right. The bones stiffened in cold weather and relaxed when the days turned balmy. They cramped before he fell sick. My mother attributed many similar and wonderful traits to Billy's hand. What I remembered was how it looked lying flat across the kitchen table—the middle two fingers bent too far to the left, the nails dirty.

"That doesn't excuse him for saying you have no soul," I said.

"I think that's what he said. Maybe I don't exactly remember. Maybe he just said I was dull."

51

"It doesn't matter. He still insulted you." Over the years Billy's moods and insults had grown routine, though no more easily understood. For weeks he would be quiet, even remote, and then the smallest something would set him off. His face would darken, veins would break in thin lines across his brow, his neck. He would lean over my mother, pinning her into some small space, and yell till he was short of breath. Usually he'd pick up a nearby object—something breakable—and wave it in her face, then toss it into a sink or on the floor. As I grew up, plates, vases, knick knacks and glass figurines met similar fates. After Billy had stomped from the house, sometimes with a packed bag, my mother and I would pick up broken shards with our fingers and try to trace what had set him off. Sometimes we could. Sometimes not. All I knew for sure was that his temper was never once directed at me. It was always at my mother.

"Can I talk to you?" I leaned on one elbow, so I was looking down at her.

She aimed smoke over my head. "Don't look so serious," she said. "He'll come back. You keep telling me that."

"I'm just not sure it's good you put up with all the temper and broken glass."

"Oh, he only does that when he's mad. I think it's a male thing. Store it up, let it out in a huff. Shouldn't you know more about that than me?"

"We're talking about you, though. He always gets the upper hand when he walks out."

She sat up then, to face me. "I have a feeling that's not all you're saying."

"Maybe we should drop it now." I was no fool, I saw how her brows had lowered and her eyes narrowed for a possible argument.

"Not just yet," and my mother slipped the joint between my

fingers, so hers would be free for gestures. "It's not the easiest thing to leave someone you've been living with for years. Isn't that what you're suggesting?"

"Sometimes a relationship just turns unhealthy." I couldn't help saying that, because I felt I should have said it a long time ago. "It's sad, sure, but there's nothing you can do. You need to see that and move on."

"Don't be so simple," she said, shaking her head like I'd disappointed her. "Is that why you came here? To talk down Billy?" She took the joint back and, pulling her knees to her chest, turned away from me.

"Like I said, I'm willing to drop it," I mumbled. "I shouldn't have brought it up." Although even then, knowing I'd set something off in her, I still couldn't soften my opinion of Billy. "I just worry sometimes," I added. "That you deserve better than he's giving you."

But by then it was too late to appease her with explanations. Did I know how Billy's hand had come to break so thoroughly it could feel the change in seasons? Did I know why she'd decided to marry him in the first place? "You were so young when we got married, you have no idea the way things were between us," she said.

We were quiet after that. She sat with her back still turned away, though by then she'd also begun rocking back and forth, and in the silence between us, I sensed she was preparing to tell me something she hoped would redeem Billy in my eyes. So I waited while she smoked and stared into the kitchen, though what exactly she was looking at, I didn't know.

According to my mother, Billy broke his hand during a cold and violent winter much like this one. She could remember vividly the details of that winter—how tired she grew of breathing through woolen scarves, of passing birds and squirrels dead in snow drifts, their mouths leaking slow blood. Trucks skidded off highways and toppled into ditches, where they remained until spring; cars died in garages and resisted jump starts; old people felt the cold move under their clothes and blankets and reach for their hearts. One night a young bartender drove home drunk on his own wine, parked in front of his house, and passed out at the wheel. When he woke in the morning, his feet had frozen to dead weight inside his boots. Both feet were amputated.

And into that winter my mother flung herself one Friday night, when the snow rode the wind and dumped drifts high against Billy's house. This was before she'd married him but after they'd dated for a few months. They drank gin and tonics in his dark living room while I slept at her apartment with a babysitter in the kitchen.

"I was scared crazy when I ran off that night," my mother told me, as if this were a truth she'd only recently come by. "Sure I'd been drinking, but mostly I was scared over Billy. How mad he got. I'd never really seen him out of control like that." But how was she to know that talking about past lovers would set him off so? They'd been giddy from gin, were sitting close and confiding; she'd foolishly thought she could tell him anything. So she told him about the time my father had taken her to a fraternity dance and, while sneaking sips of bourbon, she spilled down the front of her dress. My father walked her back to her dorm room. They'd attended a church-affiliated school where girls were expected to be discreet, but that didn't stop them from a little making out. She remembered his skin hot and moist through his white shirt, how her own skin prickled as he stroked her, his fingers whispering her name instead of his mouth. After that night, they couldn't get enough of each other. They'd finally dropped out of college to make a go of it. Was there anyone in Billy's past who'd moved under his skin that way? my mother wanted to know.

Billy was silent for a moment. Once, he admitted reluctantly. He'd been working on his own since he was sixteen, so maybe he'd never had as much time for fooling around. But yes, there was a time a few years back when he'd stopped for a hitcher while driving cross-country in a pick-up filled with vegetables. The girl rode through several states with him. They spent nights together in the back of the truck, surrounded by corn and softening potatoes. When they made love her leg would jam up and down and, once, knocked a pile of potatoes that rained down on his bare back. Just when he began to feel close to her, though, she snuck away one night and he never saw her again.

In retrospect, my mother supposed she could have salvaged the night if she'd sensed they were on delicate ground and steered the conversation in another direction. Instead, moved by Billy's tale, she'd clutched his hand tighter while more sad and silly memories rushed back to her. If she was going to be honest, she told Billy, my father hadn't even been her first. Two boys beat him to it! Daryl was her true blue first, in a shack full of teens horny on their first drunk. While she and Daryl made out, so did half the shack. Chances were good someone would moan at the same time you did. And with Jeff—

Billy sat up then, muttering.

What is it? my mother asked.

He picked up the clock on the end table. It shined in his hand, a round ball of light.

It's about time we hit the bar, if we're going at all, Billy said, and walked into the bathroom to shave.

A little disheartened, my mother finished her drink alone, then went into the bedroom to slap a brush through her hair.

Billy was still not out of the bathroom, so she peeked her head in, saw him staring at the running faucet water. He turned to her, his eyes hard and dry. A white beard of shaving cream lined his jaw.

Billy? my mother said.

He leaned her into a corner and waved his razor in her face.

Maybe you could tell me straight out what you're trying to do to me, he said. Then I'll at least know what I'm up against.

She stared back at him, his face a blur before her, razor lingering just beneath her eye. She shook her head but couldn't speak.

A boyfriend here, a man there, he said. I suppose you're trying to tell me something with all these roving leg stories. I suppose they mean something.

That was years ago, she finally whispered.

No, I don't think so. You just finished talking about it. It must still be on your mind. Now it's on my mind too. Is that what you were after? Is that it?

His voice had grown loud. He tossed his razor into the sink and grabbed her arm in a way that pinched a nerve. A dry panicky lump rose in her throat. What had come over him? His face was flushed with hot blood, his breath smelled too sharp and thick with gin. Finally he backed away, gripped the sink with both hands, and continued staring into the still-running faucet water while trying to catch his breath. She took this opportunity to rush from the bathroom, grab her coat and run from the house. She almost slammed into Billy's snowmobile as she lurched across the lawn through the deepening snow. Billy opened a window and leaned out.

Don't think I'm coming after you, he yelled. Don't think I'm fool enough to come after you in this storm, pretty lady.

She hurried toward her apartment, leaving her scarf behind and not caring. She wouldn't go back. She'd never seen him like that before and never wanted to again. In those few cold minutes of confused walking, she decided that as soon as she'd saved enough money, she would move away from this town for good. She wanted to forget winters that flattened her lungs and froze the breath in her nose. Forget her lingering dreams of my father, how his body must have arced against the sky as he dropped from the collapsed church roof scaffolding, a hammer still in hand. And of course forget Billy, after what she'd just seen. Wherever she moved would be a warm place, with palm trees and low flat buildings and drinks with colorful umbrellas perched along the sides. She would lie on the beach for days and let the sun shine between her legs. The men would have dark skin, white teeth and soft voices. Preferably they wouldn't speak English.

She finally entered downtown and passed shops, restaurants, insurance companies, all with black empty windows. She stopped in front of the VFW bar, its small window sign flickering dream-red. She hadn't planned to stop at the bar, but what the hell? There was still time before the babysitter had to leave and my mother wanted a drink. Billy wouldn't approve of her drinking alone and that cemented her decision. She swung the door wide. She was, after all, a widow, barely turned thirty.

The bar was dim. Cigarette smoke clung to the air, a screen between her and the rest of the room. Only a few people were drinking on a night like this. Two men sat on bar stools, apart from each other. Both looked up when she entered, then dropped their sullen eyes back to their beer mugs. Sometimes my mother wondered about moody men who drank alone in the VFW. She imagined they were veterans of some recent or distant war, who drank to forget more than fights they'd had with their wives or girlfriends. Once they'd carried heavy guns on their shoulders and used them to kill men, women, babies, dogs. They'd bombed villages, dodged explosives that spilled color and gas into the air, waded chest deep in rivers and swamps thick with corpses floating face down, breathed the smell of blood in the air, bled themselves. That was why they were so despondent. Something wild and extreme had happened to them far away from home, in a place she'd never been. They couldn't look so lost and confused simply over stupid lovers quarrels.

A young couple sat in a corner booth under a Budweiser sign. My mother could tell they were fighting. She understood the young man's stern clenched jaw, the girl's turned head so no one would notice her swollen face and red stuffy nose. My mother ordered a beer and sat in a booth away from the bickering young couple, but near the corner table where a man sat alone, sneaking hits off a joint. His beard had a wet slick animal look. He was almost tall, with thick muscles and dark knotty hair that gripped his skull like shallow brush. If she remembered correctly, his name was Jacob Something or other. As a teenager he'd wrestled his way to high school fame. She remembered grainy photos of him in the local paper, his thick bull's neck sporting medals given in honor of him leaving yet another opponent pinned and kicking against the mat. She leaned toward Jacob's table. If she was alone, she would think and be weakened.

Could I have a hit? she asked him. Those were hippie times and everyone was happy to share their drugs, even in nothing small towns.

Sure, he said, and handed her the joint under the table. She inhaled, watched him. He seemed shy in his smelly farmer's flannel shirt. He didn't speak while she smoked his joint away in full view of the bartender, who either didn't notice or didn't care to.

Finally she handed the cigarette back and asked Jacob if he'd been a high school wrestling star. Won titles, perfected some leg lock, shaken a young boy's brain to mush, anything?

Jacob smiled then, teeth showing in his beard.

I was state champion a few years ago, he said.

Yes, my mother said. I remember now. You were very good.

I believe I still hold several school records, he pointed out.

In fact, he said his teammates had nicknamed him Rake, because they relied on him to bring in the most points and medals. My mother listened while he detailed some of his most remarkable wins. She had nothing to offer and nothing better to do. Jacob helped her forget Billy. The beer alone wasn't enough. She concentrated on his words like they were shapes in the air, though she would have preferred not hearing about shattered jaws and dislocated shoulders.

The young couple stood up suddenly. My mother stared at the long bright braid that hung down the girl's back, at the school letter jacket the boy still wore but had outgrown. They walked into the snow side by side, without touching. My mother turned to Jacob and asked if he'd like to dance? There was no dance floor so they pushed away a few tables. The song my mother chose on the silver jukebox had a loud swift beat. The bartender and two lonely vets watched while she swayed her hips and sidled across the sticky floor, feeling young and conspicuous, wishing only that she was wearing a skirt so she could swirl it around her legs. Jacob moved his arms through the air as though he was readying himself for an attack from behind.

My mother learned a few things that night. She learned that one dance raised her out of her drunkenness enough so that

59

she felt suddenly more alert. She stared at Jacob, remembered she barely knew him, and stopped dancing. She thought of Billy's luminous eyes, his skin rough and tense against hers. She shivered.

She learned she'd misjudged Jacob. He wasn't shy. That night, if anything, he was stupidly in love. After the dance he kissed her by the lighted jukebox, his lips flattening her mouth against her face. When he was through she sat back down in the booth and Jacob slid in beside her. He said he had an aunt in Kentucky who wrapped her head in scarves and read palms for a living. She'd taught him how to predict a person's destiny by the curve of a line. If my mother wanted, they could drive his pick-up back to his house in the country by a frozen lake, and he would read her future under the lampshade. While he spoke he caressed one of her hands. She tried to close her fingers, but his thumb was pressed into her palm. He raised the hand to his mouth and kissed it, slipping his tongue between his lips. She watched him do this. The hand did not seem like hers so she could not draw it away.

And she learned that Billy could not leave her outside in a snowstorm. Or in a bar, with a man reading her palm with his tongue. First she stared at Jacob's bowed curly head, then looked up as Billy sat in the booth, his face wet with melted snow. He wore no hat or gloves, only his parka. A pinch of shaving cream that had survived the snow and cold still spotted his neck. His nose ran and silvered his upper lip. He brushed his nose with the back of his hand.

Sorry to bother everyone on such a fine evening, he said. I'm here to take this no doubt drunken woman home with me.

Jacob stared at Billy. He still held my mother's hand, his thumb pressed into her lifeline.

And quit petting her palms, Billy said. Your hands are filthy.

Jacob dropped her hand against the table.

The bartender rattled a knife in a glass to announce last call.

My mother pushed her way from the booth. When she stood, she swayed.

What the hell do you think you're doing here? she asked Billy. I was having a fine time without you. Rake can read my palms whenever he wants.

Be quiet, Billy said through his teeth.

My mother said, This pair of roving legs was having a perfectly good time. I'm waiting for Rake here to predict how many happy years I have ahead of me with you out of my life.

Billy said, Shut up you're making a scene.

Jacob wanted to know who the fuck Billy thought he was, first insulting Jacob's hands and then telling this poor woman to shut up.

Billy didn't look at Jacob. He looked at my mother. She felt dizzy.

Jacob reached across the booth and grabbed Billy's collar with one big wrestler's hand. Their arms flailed for a second, then Billy's knuckles smashed accidentally against Jacob's mouth.

I'm not in the mood for any of this, Billy said.

My mother made a break for it. She stumbled through the bar smoke and back into the night. Wind caught under her unbuttoned coat and snapped it behind her like a cape. She turned down an empty street and ran, her feet slowed in the snow and ice. Dimly she heard Billy's snowmobile jump to life and turn the corner after her.

She ran harder, faster, knowing it was no good. She was

bound to him, somehow, in a way she couldn't escape, didn't have the strength to break. She ran until her side pinched and her breath sharpened in her throat. Billy's snowmobile headlights shined her down. He killed the roaring engine and ran the last few yards himself, his boots crunching snow. Someone turned on a light in the house across the street as she hurried onto the slick sidewalk.

Damn you, she said when Billy grabbed her elbow and turned her around. Damn you.

We're going home now, Billy said in a quiet way. Come on. Stop this.

He leaned forward and tried to kiss her. She bit his lips. She tried hitting his chest, but her arms were pinned against her side by his embrace. His leg was jammed between hers and she felt him growing hard.

Damn! she screamed again. He screamed it back at her, two times loud into her face, so that she swallowed the breath of his yell and choked. He shook her once. They pressed tight against each other, still struggling. A woman from the lighted house opened the door a crack and peered out.

At that same moment they went down. My mother fell straight back, the sky in a sudden spin of darkness around her. Billy pitched on top of her, his arms still locked in an embrace. Before they landed his hands cupped the back of her skull. She felt his hands shiver when they hit the ice. She heard the singular clean snap of bone.

As soon as she caught her breath she rolled over and away, suddenly silent. Billy held up his hand, two middle fingers bent down like icicles. Then he pulled himself on his knees to the snowmobile, leaned against the machine, and cried.

The woman in the house shut her door when she saw Billy crying.

My mother stood up and stared at Billy curled against the snowmobile, cradling his injured hand against himself.

I'm sorry, she whispered, kneeling beside him. His hand looked large and dark, the skin already tinged a drowned blue. She touched one of his fingers with her breath held.

Billy, she said, these fingers are broken. We have to go to a doctor.

He shook his head. No, he whispered. Not now. It's late.

We can't just wait until morning, if your hand is broken.

Let's just go back, he panted. Please. Let's just go home.

She said she had to get back to me and the sitter, but that Billy should come and spend the rest of the night with her.

She helped him onto the snowmobile, his breath puffing jags of mist at her neck. She drove carefully down the street, steering the machine the way Billy had shown her at the start of the winter, when he'd guided her through ditches and across fields. Now the wind had slowed and the snowfall was thinning. Behind her Billy rested his chin between her shoulder blades, dipped his injured hand into her coat pocket.

And that night, after they hastily dismissed the babysitter, they stripped off their clothes and lay under blankets until morning. Together, their bodies created a tunnel of warmth that extended the full length of the bed. My mother curled into this warmth. She raised the wrist of Billy's injured hand, still winter-cold, and placed his swollen fingers against one of her breasts. In the warmth and the quiet, his tears disappeared. He breathed deep. Trains rattled in the distance, a forlorn shaking sound in the cold night. She blocked the sound out. She lay her head against his chest instead, listening to the steady knocking of his heart between his ribs. Billy fell asleep with his mouth in her hair, whispers stilled on his lips.

They married soon after that. Billy wore a hand splint for a couple of weeks, and his fingers healed, though not completely, of course. He told her once that he didn't care. Baby, he said, it's the smallest expense in the world to pay, to win back love.

By the time my mother was through, she'd moved out to the kitchen and leaned her forehead against the window. She peered through a small circle in the iced-over glass, waiting for the lights of Billy's car. The gloves drooped at her chest where she held them. She said what I didn't understand, though she certainly hoped I would someday, was that Billy loved her as much as she loved him. In some strange way he might love her more. But his was a hopeless love, the kind that bared teeth when it broke through his surface of quiet and indifference. I was young and foolish it I thought she could simply run from what had rooted between them over so many years.

There wasn't much left for me to say, though it also seemed I shouldn't let it end there. But we were both tired, it was late, and though Billy still wasn't home, she'd calmed some and I didn't want to upset her again. "Let's not talk anymore, Mom," I said. "Ok? Let's just watch the video."

Ten minutes into it, she fell asleep on the sofa, the TV's light catching in her hair. I sat on the floor beside her and sucked the last breath from the joint. For awhile I thought about Billy and what my mother had told me. I tried to picture him charging after her on a snowmobile, his eyes blazing in his forehead, and how his fingers had snapped while curled around her head. Then I thought about Sharon and realized I couldn't remember precisely what she looked like. We'd been apart for a month after living together for nearly a year, and already her face was blurred and small in my mind. I might have been remembering her through water. I thought her eyes had been hazel but they may have been brown, or blue or green, they might have been any color. I concentrated, hard, until the back of my eyes stung from pressure, and still I couldn't pull her face from shadow into full focus. This made me feel so cold and empty inside that my joint-hand shook and I rested it against my knee.

And when Billy's car pulled into the garage an hour later in that long night, my mother was awake and at the door, waiting to meet him. He walked into the kitchen, his face and hands raw. He said hello and I nodded back, unsure what to say now that I knew this small secret part of his life that had changed my mother's forever. I felt I was seeing him for the first time, standing in the open doorway with a light film of snow blowing over his boots. I watched my mother and Billy in the kitchen, facing each other, not speaking. Billy shut the door. "It took you long enough to notice you forgot your gloves," my mother said finally, very low, and lay them on the table.

Billy picked them up, then walked into the bathroom. While he was gone, my mother turned on the kitchen water faucet until a light steam rose. When he returned, pushing an aspirin tablet under his tongue, she took his hands and placed them under the running water. Billy let her do this. They still didn't say a word.

I had come back to tell my mother to leave a man who was no good for her, but I ended up sitting in that dark corner of the living room, apart from them, watching my mother and Billy warm their hands in water. I didn't stare at them with envy, really, but something closer to wonder, and maybe fear too. Wonder at how their kind of love just kept going, instinctively and without limits, and would continue on like that through all the fading years of their lives. Fear that I would never know that kind of love. Or that I would.

Private Room

The boy has never wanted much. Or rather, he can live without most ordinary comforts, but what he does want, he needs, obsessively and without question.

His own room, for one. It's his greatest longing. By the time he's fourteen, he's grown tired of life in a small box-sized house with his father and mother and two round-shouldered brothers. They live side by side, unavoidably together, yet haven't, it seems to the boy, much to say to one another. Often they bump into each other, or they bruise their hips against furniture or walls while passing in the narrow rooms and hallways. No one speaks when this happens. They back off and suffer their stinging sides in private.

Sometimes the boy imagines the air inside the house smells like all their breaths, combined. The smell is neither pleasant nor unpleasant, but it is stale, and unchanging, somewhat like the smell of a seldom used closet. At times the boy would prefer not breathing at all to inhaling the collective breath of his family. Of course, he can't indulge such thoughts for long.

His father is the only one with a room of his own, and he's dying. It will be a long slow process, this dying, so the doctors have allowed him to live his final months in the privacy of his home. The family has adapted to this. The boy's mother visits the room often, tending to her husband's needs, but sleeps on a cot in the living room where the TV used to be. The TV has been moved to the father's room and placed on a clean spot atop the dresser. The two brothers open doors for their father, though he's quite capable of managing this on his own, or they join him on walks, in case his strength gives out before he can make it back inside for his pills. The boy alone is having problems. If his father joins them at the supper table, he can't eat. If they're alone in a room, the boy's throat thickens and he could not speak even if there were a reason to. He sees his father's newly thin arms, speckled skin, deflating chest. He pictures how his father's lungs must look, inside that chest—black, softly caving inward, eaten away slowly by an irreversible germ. All the boy can think is that he must not get too near.

And he cannot help envying his father a private room. It seems wrong to envy a dying man this, especially when the man is also his father, but the boy can't dictate his feelings. He shares a room with his two brothers, Hal and Sid. Both are very protective of it. The older, Hal, will push the boy onto the bed and make mysterious, random threats when he wishes to be alone. "Microbe, you have entered my region," he whispered once, leaning wide-eyed over the boy while brandishing an invisible sword. "So you're mine now. You belong to me like property."

Sid talks less, but is prone to slapping the boy or yanking the boy's hair if he wants the room to himself. The boy alone does not shove, pull, or hit. He doesn't like violence; fears it, really.

70

He reads a lot—literature, science fiction, prize-winning short story volumes—and violence is rarely promoted. Acts of violence, he has learned, blemish a person, each act a personal failure that diminishes you, bit by bit. So the boy usually just walks from the room, pretending he doesn't mind.

At night, though, he often lies awake, the air clogged with the sounds of his brothers' sleep, and imagines himself living in another place, away from here. He imagines a large private room inside a very large white house overlooking a lake. The house is run by a kindly older woman, someone like his mother but less sad, less burdened by the everyday. The house has several rooms, all for rent at affordable rates. The boy doesn't know what he'll do in his room, though he does believe it will be quiet there. He'll probably read, think, live inside this serene personal space. If he likes, he can walk along the beach, listen to the water lapping, and scavenge for shells.

This is what the boy wants, though at fourteen he can't have it. So he settles for moving into the barn loft one spring day. It's bright, a liquid sun eyeing him from between the budding tree branches. He manages his move in three trips. He moves out blankets, several books and magazines, a transistor radio and a flashlight. He brings a deck of cards because he's quite good at solitaire. He also takes his pillow, a small wash basin he scrubs thoroughly, a clean wash rag, and a bar of soap. The boy wants to remain clean, though he'll be living in a barn where things are generally unclean. Fortunately the barn has a hand pump, so he'll always have fresh water nearby, though he'll still have to go inside to eat and use the bathroom. *It's not perfect*, the boy thinks, *but you always start somewhere.*

For the first couple weeks, no one seems to notice his general absence from the house. The boy has never felt more free. The barn is wide, high, airy, and the hay in the corner is clean enough.   At night he hears sounds that possibly should scare him, though he's not afraid.   He hears boards creaking, pigeons cooing, bats snapping their wings.   At unexpected moments, he clicks on his flashlight and watches the bats flutter outside the beam.   The boy knows that bats lack vision—their movement is directed by the sound of echo—so he has never understood why they fly outside the light, or even know it's there.   Is light itself sound?   Or is all of this coincidence, or worse, a faulty understanding on his part?

He's pondering these things one day when his mother climbs the six-rung ladder into the loft and sits down beside him.   Her breathing is hard and sonorous.   The boy feels responsible; she wouldn't have climbed into the loft otherwise.   She's no longer the trim woman from his childhood who laughed frequently though never indiscriminately, and wore her hair in loose, stylish perms.   Now her hair is grey and tightly permed. She holds a yellow dish towel wound around her hand like a bandage.   "This is your home these days, schnook?" she asks.

Schnook.   The boy can't remember when his mother first called him this.   Hal and Sid have names, but he is schnook.

He shrugs.   "It's sort of neat up here," he says.

"Your father's begun to wonder," she says.   "You're so scarce these days.   I always tell him you're around, he must have just missed you."

The boy stares as a barn swallow weaves among the rafters, hangs in air for a moment, then swoops in a hard dip back out the barn door.

"If you tell me what I can do to make things—easier—on you, I'll give it a try," she says, her eyes growing more round as the boy watches.   "I certainly will try."

He says, "There's nothing.   I like it out here."

"Schnook, why?   What have we done?"

Her question is earnest and places great pressure on the boy. He pictures his mother's heart pumping pink and fragile in his open hands.

"I'm camping," he says. "It's sort of like camp, really. I'm seeing how long I can get by on the basics."

This answer restores his mother's color. "Well, that's fine then," she says. "If this is an education for you, schnook, I won't complain. I only wanted you to know I'll do anything I can."

The boy can't explain there's nothing she can do. Some needs—yearnings—reach beyond human intercession.

Two days later, Hal sticks his head into the loft and says, "You're a fuckin' queer one, microbe. Do you know what you're doing to them, sitting up here? They think they've done something. Pop thinks it's because he's sick."

The boy wants to protest, yet offhand can't think of a defense.

"There's one way to redeem yourself," Hal says. "One. You can get off your ass and come back inside with me now."

The boy stares evenly at his brother. A tiny bead of sweat gleams on Hal's temple. The boy feels sad about that.

Hal climbs one rung higher, so his full torso is now in the loft. "Of course, that's asking too much. I knew it. You don't think about a single living soul other than yourself, isn't that right?" He thumps two knuckles against the boy's rather narrow chest. "Is there a heart in there somewhere, microbe?"

The boy considers this question for most of the afternoon. Often he'll feel he deserves what is said to him, but he's fairly certain he did not deserve this. In early evening, he's distracted by the sound of voices in the yard. He peers though a crack between the boards. All his family is outside surrounding the father, who's sitting in a wicker chair to watch the fabulous sunset—orange and yellow and red streaking the distant sky, birds passing over the house, flying toward the color. His family seems reasonably happy without him, the boy thinks. He should turn away now that he understands this, but he doesn't turn away. He watches until the sun has disappeared and he can no longer see them, though he can still hear their voices, laughing and calling each other by name in the dark.

When he's fifteen, the boy hitches to town one night, secretively, the darkness his shield, and buys a ticket to the Twin Cities.

This is three months after his father has died. Now is as good a time as any to leave, the boy thinks—possibly better, because his own absence will be diminished by the recent, larger loss of his father. His mother and brothers will feel less pain over his departure now than at any other time. Or so he tells himself.

They buried his father in a weedy plot behind the Lutheran church. The boy lived in the house with his family for several days after the funeral, but they eyed him uncomfortably, a stranger sharing their grief. He knew then he would leave.

He has received a modest sum of money from his father's death; with this, he intends to find his own place and begin again.

He leaves his mother a note, attempting explanation. *I'm going off to take care of myself,* the boy writes. *You won't have to worry about me. I'll return someday to visit you.* He places this note on a clean plate and sets it in front of where she normally sits for breakfast.

In the bus station, he tries not to linger on the past. He's embarking on a journey toward something more than he has now, and he wants to trust this impulse. The station is small, nearly empty, just the boy and an old woman with her head rested against the Pepsi machine and a man behind the counter, paging idly through a magazine the boy can't see. No one will recognize him here. It's past midnight, and everyone the boy knows is most likely asleep.

On the chair beside him lies a small yellow pamphlet with a dove carrying an olive branch in its beak. FOUR EASY STEPS TO SPIRITUAL HAPPINESS, the pamphlet reads. He crumbles it in his hand and, because he can't litter and there are no trash cans nearby, dips it into his pocket. Simple solutions are dishonest, he thinks, yet seductive. They're easy fodder for the spiritually hungry. *I must be very careful,* he tells himself.

When the bus arrives, the boy sits near the back, the only passenger for six rows. He has an urge to spread his arms wide and touch nothing, but he doesn't really do this. Instead he watches the town pass—street lamps and dark slumbering houses and office buildings with no signs of life inside their lighted windows. He's lived in this town since he was a baby. He can't help feeling nostalgic, though he doesn't feel regret. In fact, beneath his shirt, he's sure his heart must be expanding to accommodate this new freedom.

Later, he dreams in small snatches. In one dream he's lying on a bed inside a black room, a body, then he turns to vapor and rises outside himself. He twists under the bed and coils between the bed springs. The boy wakes feeling sadly concrete. A young woman wearing nylons sits in the seat across from him. Her hair is straight and an average brown, except for the strands tucked behind her ears, which have been blasted violet.

The moment he opens his eyes she lights a match to the cigarette between her lips. Smoke is released. "This is the smoking section," she says defensively. "I'm allowed."

The boy nods. He doesn't care if she smokes—there are more important issues to occupy him—though it's true smoke irritates him when he's not deep inside his thoughts. He does care that she's sitting so near him when many other empty seats are available, a discreet distance away. He shuts his eyes and leans back, pretending to doze, but the young woman is undeterred. "I could never sleep on a bus," she says. "I can't sleep, period. I've been an insomniac since I was a kid."

Again the boy nods. Behind his closed lids he sees tiny specks of red light, spinning like planets before they fade into black. The world is filled with lonely people, he thinks. There are worse things than listening to one.

"Insomniacs tend to worry," she says. "Whatever you've heard about us is true. We're impatient. We can't sleep until we've solved every one of our problems. Of course, we never really solve them, so consequently, we never sleep."

The boy rarely has problems sleeping. Sleep is one place he can go alone without feeling shame. Maybe this is why the girl's eyes carry a dull, bludgeoned look. She's can't escape hard reality. The boy knows this can kill, and often does. Once he read a book about a future guerilla society who injected its prisoners with drugs that eliminated their ability to dream or imagine. Reality became their entire existence. He finds this idea frightening, even more frightening than trying to picture eternity. Some things, unfiltered, are too harsh for the human mind to endure.

Eventually the bus enters the city. The boy is fully awake now and stares out the glass, at bridges and freeways yielding to narrow streets. Huge glass buildings tower above the tiny bus as it maneuvers and turns, confidently aimed for where it will end up. The boy's legitimate excitement is nothing too dizzying or obvious, though. He pretends he's any cool customer returning home to the city.

"You stare," the girl says, "like you've never seen a city before."

The boy doesn't answer.

He lives inside the bus terminal for nearly a week. This terminal is larger and more crowded than the one in his home town. Sometimes, he guesses, a hundred or more people are inside at once, walking through the revolving glass doors, carrying suitcases and boxes and bulky wrinkled purses, walking with their arms latched together, as if they haven't seen each other in a long while or are expecting to never see each other again. Others, like the boy, stare ahead, a little dazed, with no one to greet them.

He makes himself at home in a far corner chair, the suitcase by his feet. Nearby a few men and women sit hunched in their coats, picking lint off their sleeves or scanning abandoned newspapers or staring with only mild interest at quarter-fed TV sets. They do not know each other and do not try to. Eventually, a disengaged voice will announce a certain bus and one or more of them stand, relieved. The boy, of course, is always waiting. He pretends his bus has not yet arrived and he's expecting a long wait. In the evenings he finds a couple empty chairs and lies across them, removing his coat so it can serve as a blanket. But surprisingly, he can't sleep well here. Someone is always awake, always moving and staring. Once he closes his eyes, he feels he's being watched, that something he doesn't intend to show is showing anyway. His eyes fly open, though no one is ever paying him special attention.

His food supply comes largely from the terminal vending machines. He eats nuts dusted with brittle salt. He eats chips and honey candy and fire balls. Sometimes he'll buy a cup of soup or a hamburger that can be quickly warmed in an easy-to-manage microwave. Other times, he secures his suitcase inside a locker and walks into the city, looking for a small cafe with specials advertised on cardboard in the windows. Once he ate a fluffy omelette at a diner shaped like a boxcar. Always, though, he returns, a little anxiously, to the terminal where his suitcase waits.

The boy knows he can't continue like this for long. It's not what he'd pictured or wanted for himself in the loft. But he doesn't know how to go about getting his own room. The paper offers few rooming opportunities within his modest budget.

By the fifth night, the boy's dreams turn fitful. He's standing in a crowded ticket line, pressed against tall people whose bare backs are scarred with pimples. Then he's lying on a floor and dozens of people step over him, swinging their purses and newspapers, but his tongue has swollen thick as peanut butter and he can't speak. Finally he's sitting on a chair, apart from crowds, and his father sits down beside him. The boy's heart leaps, hangs like a balloon in his chest, but his father, too, is silent. He strikes a match for a cigarette, but the flame flickers and dies. He drops the match and tries another, and another, struggling for a light. When the boy wakes, these dreams cling to him like a second skin.

The next night the boy jerks awake thinking he's in the barn loft. He says quite audibly, "What?" and leans his head sideways to hear. A middle-aged woman eyes him, startled by the sound, then gazes down at a stain on the floor. He's a tiny wrinkle in her life, as easily forgotten as the toast she's eaten for breakfast.

But one young man stares long after the woman has turned away. This person is seventeen or maybe eighteen, wiry and strong, though his features are delicate. His hair is soft and blonde and fine, his eyes the blue of electric flame. The more the boy looks, the more the young man's eyes turn blue. He wears a jaunty hat with an orange feather on the side and is cleaning his nails with a toothpick.

How can the boy sleep comfortably under such scrutiny? He can't, so he sits up, his thoughts rumbled. He misses his mother so opens his case, cautiously, and removes a yellow pad and a chewed down pencil. He's one of her sons, after all, and she has no idea where he's gone. But he can't write to her comfortably. The words sound tired and unfelt on the page. *Dear Mom,* he writes. *How are you? I'm fine, please don't worry.* Or *Dear mother, Let me first apologize for leaving.* . . . Each of these beginnings he crosses out. Words seem unable to bridge the space between where he wants to be and where is family has always been. And he can't offer details about the bus terminal. She would worry if she learned he was living out of vending machines.

Eventually the young man with the fine blond hair walks over, springing on the balls of his feet, and sits beside the boy. "I'm Jay," he says, flicking the toothpick onto the floor.

The boy nods but remains silent.

"You're smart to be writing," Jay continues. "It'll keep you alert. Sleeping's a mistake here. You'll get ripped off bigtime. This place is crawling with weirdos. Heathens. I mean it."

The boy smiles at that. Heathens! He's very curious about Jay now, though he's unsure how to keep the conversation going. He hasn't talked to anyone, really, for days. Jay's his first.

"Are you waiting for a bus?" Jay asks.

"Yes," the boy answers, because the question seems harmless enough.

"You're a liar," Jay says lightly. The boy stiffens, the accusation making him alert. "You've been here a couple days, at least. I've seen you. I keep my eyes open." He grins and rubs a knuckle across one eye. "So what're you doing here? No more crapping me."

"How would you know I've been here that long unless you have too?"

"Don't you got nowhere to go?"

"Don't you?" the boys asks. *I'm on my own now,* he thinks. *I have to be careful.*

"I got a place," Jay says. "I don't need to live here, that's for sure. I come to keep current on the rates. As soon as I scrape some dollars together, I'm heading for Arizona. No one needs to sell me on the desert." Jay's been in the city for a few months, as it turns out, but he's tired of its offerings, and winter is nearing. "Winter slows everyone down," he says. "It's like hibernation, except you're awake enough to know you're cold and miserable." He removes a second toothpick from his shirt pocket and jabs it into his mouth. The boy pictures winter as a snow monster that swallows the state whole and holds it inside his frozen mouth until spring. "Cold is bullshit, if you ask me," Jay adds. "At least there's sun in Arizona."

The boy listens while Jay talks his theories and shifts his gaze back and forth, twitching with an energy that comes from deep inside him, or so the boy thinks. Jay talks as if he, too, has not spoken in a long while. The boy can't help feeling good about this, chosen in some way.

Finally Jay stops talking and leans back in his chair, folding his arms. He studies the boy's threadbare coat, worn jeans, stiff shirt. The boy worries about his week's worth of smells. "Winter's almost here," Jay says. "Three weeks at the most. You can't live in a terminal forever. That's not practical."

The boy doesn't answer.

"That's what you're doing here, isn't it? Living here?"

The boy doesn't answer.

"You don't have nowhere else to go. That's my bet. You don't got no one and nothing."

The boy doesn't answer a third time. That isn't completely true, is it?

Satisfied, Jay leans back in his chair. He removes the toothpick and rams the reverse end into his mouth. "You're a runaway," he says. "I got eyes."

And still the boy is silent, though he wants to speak now. For the first time, someone has seen beneath his surface to where the truth of him lies. There's a pleasure in this, the boy thinks, a warmth in feeling known and connected.

"So what if I am?" he asks.

And later, with the sun only a scrape in the east, Jay mentions a hospital that rents rooms to boarders.

"They have a whole wing of rooms for a steal," he says. According to Jay, this hospital has run upon hard times. It has more rooms than patients; this waste is reflected in their budget sheets. A few years ago, by grouping their sick together on the same floors, the hospital discovered an entire unused wing. These rooms rent charitably at $100 a month. "They can't change more than that," he says. "They got connections with a church."

The boy tries not to show his excitement; for whatever reasons, he feels this wouldn't be wise. But he can't help asking a hurried question: "Do you think I could get a room there?"

Jay squints. He's not looking at the boy now, instead is moving his lips slightly, as if debating with someone unseen. The boy waits, wishing he could hear. "You'll need an in," Jay says at last. "For insurance. I could maybe be that in. I lived in one of them rooms myself a few months ago. You Catholic?"

The boy confesses he's Lutheran.

"Won't matter," Jay says. "They can't discriminate." Again Jay looks at him, steadily, eyes so purely blue they encourage trust. "I could show you there if you're sure you want to go."

"Yes," the boy says.

"If you're sure you want this service from me."

"Let's rock," the boy says, feeling funny and spry. He believes in good things so much in this moment that, when Jay reaches down to carry the suitcase, the boy lets him.

Once outside, the boy feels something's wrong, though he can't immediately pinpoint what. At first he tries to ignore this feeling. He concentrates on their walk, searching for anything out of place. Traffic is scarce, the sidewalks empty. It's barely morning. They cross streets and shortcut through unused parking lots, pass banks and restaurants and clothing stores. Mannequins pose in the still-darkened windows, their sole purpose for existence to be seen. Soon his attention wanders back to Jay, walking several feet ahead with the suitcase. Each sneakered step slaps the pavement, hard and fierce. The wind nudges Jay's hat, rocks it, and finally snatches it off completely, flinging it into the boy's chest. He catches it and holds it out for Jay, but Jay doesn't acknowledge he knows the hat is gone, so the boy carries it and continues following.

Jay is different, the boy sees at last. He's walking too fast, his pace is impatient, his shoulders too rigidly held. The boy doesn't know what's caused this change. The cold wind penetrating Jay's light jacket? The waking city with its smells and annoyances? Or had the boy said something off-putting? He doesn't think so, but he can't be sure. Sometimes, his nature and desires alone drive people to scorn and aggression. He has no control over this.

Finally Jay leads him through a narrow alley filled with trash cans, boxes ripped open by the mouths of dogs. "This isn't the way," the boy mumbles, only half convinced by his own skepticism. He's afraid Jay plans to run off with his suitcase. "It's a short cut," Jay answers. "Don't have a hernia."

They walk farther into the alley, the shuffle of their sneakers the only sounds. Then, almost at the other end, Jay stops abruptly and they stand very still, as if they've always been there. "Now just circle the corner," Jay says. "Wait on the steps. When someone comes to open up, tell them you want to rent."

"Sure," the boy says, without joy. He's very confused. An odd grayness has settled around them. The sky is gray, the clouds fronting the feeble early morning sun are gray. Jay's cheeks in profile are gray. "Aren't you coming?" the boy asks. "To introduce me?"

Jay shakes his head. Buildings rise above them, the hospital rises, but they are the only people. A sheet of newsprint circles the corner, dances in the air, tangles playfully around Jay's feet. He kicks it away and stomps on it.

The boy knows then he's been misled.

"You can do it yourself," Jay says. "You're not helpless, are you? I got my own life." He shifts his feet in the dust. One sneaker is untied, the boy notices dimly. Jay holds out one sweaty palm. "That's twenty bucks please."

The boy stares without comprehension.

"Twenty bucks," Jay repeats, wagging his hand. "You didn't think I do this shit for free, did you?"

The boy's there, in the alley, but feels suddenly like he's not there at all. He thinks he smells a wet dog nearby.

"You didn't suppose I come for free?" Jay leans the boy against the hospital wall; the boy feels cold concrete through his jacket, passing between his shoulder blades. "Did you think I wouldn't cost you? Is that it?"

"I don't have that kind of money," the boy murmurs.

Jay stares away from the hospital for a moment. In the building across the street, a woman in a slip opens a window and leans out, gazing at the thin cloud of city gasses made visible by the morning light. The boy hopes she will spot them and call down, but she ducks back inside. Jay is still except for his lips, which have begun lightly moving again. If the boy reaches out now and shoves Jay, hard, like he means it, he could get away. But his suitcase is still in Jay's hand, and he can't leave it behind. Besides, he knows he won't shove Jay, not when his lips are moving that way. Instead he wants to touch Jay's lips and feel what is being said.

Without warning Jay's attention snaps back, so forcefully his head snaps backward too. "You ain't got that kind of money?" he says. "But there's another lie. I *seen* you with that kind of money. I've been watching you eat and I been watching you sleep for at least a day and maybe longer. I know you."

"I'm on a budget," the boy mumbles. "I can't afford to give away any money."

"Give away?" Jay clutches the boy's collar, though he doesn't tighten his grip. "I carried your luggage, didn't I? I walked you to your new home, didn't I? I did you a service. You owe me."

The boy can't speak. He's still far away, though he's physically closer to Jay now than he's been in all the days he's known him.

Then the boy remembers, also from far away, that he's only known Jay for two or three hours.

"I thought we were friends," the boy mumbles. "I thought you were helping me."

Jay licks his blistered upper lip. "I'm tired of this," he says, his voice thin and peaking. "I'm tired of you. Do you hear me?

84

You're stalling. You're trying to talk me out of something? What have you ever done for me? I got to get to Arizona, don't I?"

His own voice inspires him. He sets the suitcase down firmly and, with the hands of a professional, forces the boy to his knees. The boy doesn't resist. He knows this feeling—on his knees against his will—though he can't remember from where. Jay pushes his hand into the boy's back pants pocket and retrieves the wallet, his breath coming fast and furious. *I'm being robbed*, the boy thinks, and this too feels familiar. Jay rifles through the wallet, removes a twenty—his father's money, the boy remembers hastily—and tosses the wallet back at the boy. Then he grabs his hat from the boy's hands. The boy makes no move to retrieve his wallet, only stares into Jay's face. What had he seen there that had misled him?

Jay's face is pure white now, his eyes shiny and anxious. "Quit looking," he whispers and strikes the boy in the face. He doesn't need to do this for the benefit of his theft. He does this by choice. The boy will ponder Jay's reasons for this choice for years.

The boy lies in the alley for some time, unmoving, his nose cold with blood. He doesn't even lift his hands to wipe himself. He's come a long way to end up here, in a place he wasn't seeking and did not belong, any more than he belonged back in the crowded house with his sad and baffled family. He closes his eyes against the sun rising over the hospital; an image of the barn loft leaps to his mind—his wash pan and coffee pot and stack of books and his red flannel blanket covering the prickly straw. He doesn't know how to feel about these memories.

When he opens his eyes a man is standing over him. A priest, with loose black sleeves and a tight black collar circling his skinny neck. There is a look in the priest's eyes that the boy also recognizes—a grim and patient acceptance of whatever is in front of him.

He kneels down to raise the boy's head off the ground. Without knowing why, the boy closes his eyes.

The priest takes care of the technicalities. Within minutes, the boy's being led by the priest himself up four flights of stairs and into a long white hall with dozens of doors, all of them with numbers on them, most of them closed. The boy follows vaguely, staring at the cracked walls; they feel wounded to him. The boy and priest pass one door that's marginally open, but the boy can't see much, just a sink and a round dish with a bar of beige soap in it.

"Who did this to you, son?" the priest asks. His voice is soft, though against the walls, his words echo with authority. "Who left you out in that alley?"

Before the boy can answer, another door opens. The boy expects to see a young face, someone his own age or Jay's age, but this face is old. Old. The man's hair is thin and gray and slicked back with Brylcream. He's naked from the belly up, chest shrunken, stomach red and paunched. The boy turns away, flustered. "Hello Malcolm," the priest says.

The boy and priest continue down the hall. *Soon we'll stop and that will be my room,* the boy thinks, trying to feel some pleasure in this. "Did you know this person?" the priest resumes. "The one who struck you?"

The boy shrugs. "He showed me here," he says.

Near the end of the hall, the priest stops and opens a door. 544. The boy steps into a room furnished with a bed, closet, chair, dresser, sink with a mirror, and a window. The window is framed with natural wood and overlooks an elm tree, stark and leafless for the oncoming winter. Across the way is another wing of the hospital, with more rooms—rooms for the truly sick, the physically dying. The priest encourages the boy inside, but once there, they both stand awkwardly, without much to say.

"I'm glad you found us, however you did it," the priest says. "This isn't a bad place, really, until you find some place else."

The boy nods, knowing he should show more gratitude, but he can't bring himself to do this. "He took some of my money," he says suddenly. "I'm not sure how much I have left to pay for this room."

"Then you'll pay what you can manage," the priest answers. "Rent's a foolish idea, when you think about it. Paying for a natural need." He stares into the mirror at a red pimple dotting the edge of his mouth. The boy watches while the priest strokes it with his fingers. "Don't worry." The priest reaches for the knob. "You should rest."

Once he's gone, the boy sets his suitcase down and lies across the bed. The sheets are clean. The whole room is quite clean, but he doesn't feel clean inside. He feels dirty. Of course, he still has enough money to pay for the room! He lied to the priest for no real reason. He stares at the ceiling, at a crack like a stringy vein reaching across the plaster to the opposite wall. He's here now, alone in a room of his own, but this no longer feels like what he wants. He doesn't feel the peace he thought he would. It's not too late for the boy to tell the priest he has the money after all, that he'll pay the full amount like any normal boarder, but he can't be sure yet if he will do this. He may or he may not. The choice is no longer clear.

Out in the hall, the boy hears a door opening, then the sound of slippered feet shuffling, slow and labored, in his direction. Possibly it's the unexpectedly old man who peered at him, or maybe the owner of the beige soap. The boy can't account for the mixture of excitement and dread he feels. As the steps near, he imagines, tentatively, how it would be if this person stopped outside his door, knocked, introduced himself and then asked the boy his name. At this moment, the boy thinks, it is precisely what he wants.

Twilight

The evening began with Cory stealing a Hostess blueberry fruit pie from the refrigerator. The pies belonged exclusively to his father. When Cory or his mother or sister Stephanie wanted to snack, they helped themselves to the unflavored potato chips or stale fig bars in the cupboard. That night his father was in the basement with a hard-backed ledger, some receipts, and several Bic pens. Twice a month he would sit down there, alone, in one of those old wooden school desks with a top that lifted, and from the receipts would estimate how much the family was costing him. He would then record his findings in one of the ledger's several narrow columns. Each family member was paired with a different color. Cory knew this, although his father did not know he knew this. Cory's color was green. With his father in the basement, keeping books, and his mother in their bedroom, resting, Cory stood alone in the kitchen. He didn't bother worrying about Stephanie, who was seventeen and dreamy and had thoughts in her head he'd given up ever figuring out. He opened the refrigerator, grabbed a pie—leaving three—and dropped it into his jacket pocket. Then he walked out the front door.

This was early October, cold but not enough to wear gloves. Cory was sixteen and restless about something. He walked across the yard to the toolshed, his hands shoved into his pockets, the knuckles of his right hand brushing against the pie's wrapper. He wouldn't even care if his father discovered it missing, he thought to himself. Still, he walked softly on the balls of his feet with his neck sunk low into his jacket collar. He would go out to the tool shed, eat the pie in private, and come back inside.

The door was open a small way, so he just stepped through—he was pretty lean—and stood in the shed's closed space for a moment. It was twilight but darker inside the shed, so his eyes needed time to adjust. He stood still, smelling the cold metal of his father's tools, imagining tiny sounds in the corners he couldn't yet see. He saw the outline of his father's car in front of him. His father parked the car in the tool shed because it was the only place available besides the driveway, and he didn't want to leave it there, a stone-toss away from the road where drunk teens frequently passed, pressing their horns. Cory reached for the wall switch and turned on the light.

First he saw a strange bike leaning on its kickstand next to the car's hood. Then he saw Stephanie in the car's back seat. He moved two steps closer. She wasn't alone. A guy was kneeled beside her, his head against her chest. All her clothes were still on, but the guy's shirt was open and pulled down to his elbows. His chest was white, without hair or sweat. When Stephanie saw Cory she reached for the boy's head, either to shield him or pull him away. Her fingers ended up rested in his hair. "Do you mind?" she asked Cory. From inside the car her words sounded flat and hissing, like they'd been steam-ironed.

The boy looked up, startled. Cory saw the boy was Billy McGregor, who lived down the road. Once in Advanced Auto Mechanics, Billy had accidentally kneed the jack from under a car he'd been lying beneath. The car came within an inch of landing across his chest. Since then, Billy McGregor was known throughout school as Billy Jack. Now Billy Jack stumbled from Cory's father's car, banging one arm against the door as he straightened. He stood so close, Cory could smell him—something like beans and a piny aftershave. His eyes were large, frantic. Cory stepped back. "Don't look at me like that," he said.

Billy Jack opened his mouth but the words stuck. He stood with his red flannel shirt still tangled around his elbows, farmer-thick shoulders and arms quivering from the cold or, maybe, the shock of Cory's unexpected appearance.

"Billy," Stephanie said, sliding across the car's vinyl seat to the door. "Cory won't tell."

Billy Jack didn't lower his eyes, though. He stared, breath in his chest a small hard pant. It was too much for Cory. He turned away from Billy Jack, but when his eyes landed on Stephanie, still inside the car, he turned away from her too. Eventually he settled on staring at the back left tire of his father's car. It looked low on air.

"I—I didn't mean anything," Billy Jack stammered.

"Why are you telling me for?" Cory asked.

"Maybe if you left," Stephanie suggested. When Cory looked up, she rolled her eyes skyward, then nodded at the tool shed door. The look angered him. He couldn't be sure why. It had something to do with the way she wore her glasses, pushed too low on her nose, and the way she sighed while jerking her head dismissively at him.

"Take it easy, Billy Jack," Cory said, winking at him. "There's nothing wrong with a little messing around."

93

First Billy Jack's face, then his neck, flushed the red of a wrestler in a chokehold. "I apologize," he said quietly, lifting his shirt over his shoulders. Without a single other glance at Stephanie, he hopped on the bicycle and pedalled from the shed, shirt flapping behind. They watched as he crossed the ditch and wobbled onto the gravel road.

Stephanie sat in the car with her mouth open for a few dramatic seconds. "You dink," she said at last and slapped her palm down on an Algebra book lying beside her, a yellow pencil between the pages. Who did she think she was fooling, Cory wondered, Algebra in the tool shed at twilight?

"It's not my fault he ditched you," Cory mumbled, although he already felt bad about what he'd said. It had been the look in her eyes behind the glasses, though, and Billy Jack's alarm—all that visible guilt. Cory couldn't help himself. But those no longer seemed like good reasons. "I'm not taking the rap for this," he added.

She touched her chest with her chewed-down fingernails. "He didn't ditch me," she said.

"Whatever. He needs to lighten up one of these days."

"Well what you know adds up to about zero," she said.

They were quiet for a moment. She rolled up one sleeve and scratched at a vein. Then she pulled the ends of her sweater over her thin blouse and folded her arms.

"He snuck over here just to see you?" Cory asked.

"I don't see why that's so surprising," she said. "And don't think you're getting any explanation."

He waited a moment, then asked, "Are you coming out?" He held the door wide, offering his hand like a suitor. He felt he owed her something. She didn't take his hand, though, or even smile, so he eventually lowered it and sat on the edge of the car seat. When he did, his jacket pockets opened wider and he remembered the pie, so he stood back up. "Well?" he asked.

She shrugged. "Not much left to do in here, is there?" she mumbled, stepping from the car without the benefit of his hand. She was a tall gangly girl, round-shouldered from years of walking slightly slumped forward, trying to disguise her full height. When standing straight, she could look across to most boys' foreheads or, in the worse cases, down into the uneven parts of their hair. "I'd appreciate it if this didn't make it back to You Know Who," she said. "We wouldn't want to get Billy into trouble."

She was looking at Cory. Outside a dog had begun to bark across the field. The air in the shed had chilled enough to lightly frost their breath. Cory felt suddenly lonely. "I won't," he said. "I'm not the KGB."

"Then what are you doing out here?"

He would have told her about the pie, if he thought he could trust her completely, and if it hadn't seemed silly, now, to have his father's blueberry pie secretly in his pocket, a sad gesture of some kind. "The shed's not yours," Cory said. "I just came out to get a hammer. I need to use one."

She nodded and nibbled at the inside of her cheek. The way she looked, any answer he gave would have done just as well. "We weren't fooling around, if you must know," she said while Cory hesitated with his new lie, wondering if he should now go inside with the hammer, or leave it behind, or what exactly. "Do you want to know what he was doing?"

"You don't have to tell me."

"If you must know," she said, "he was listening to my heart."

Cory could think of nothing to say. Instead he stared at the table where his father's tools were spread. Two steps forward, and he was peering down at them. It gave him somewhere to look besides Stephanie. He ran his fingers over the objects there, feeling them, stirring them slightly. Nails, bolts, dried paint rollers, twists of wire.

"It's true," she said. "We went in the car just to talk. He said he liked the way I smelled. And he was *serious.* You know how he gets. He means everything."

Cory nodded but kept his eyes on the tools. He kept his fingers there too. He didn't know why he wanted to be touching them. It felt wrong, somehow. The tools were cold, hard beneath his fingers.

"Anyway, I knew he wanted to ask me something," Stephanie continued. "Something special. He was so jumpy. First we just sat together in the car. Then he got up his nerve and asked if I was feeling anything between us. I was so *nervous,* when he asked that, but I said yes, because I was, you know. I felt so odd." She shook her head, remembering this. "Then he said 'I'm so nervous my heart won't stop kicking.' He said he was shaking inside. Then he wanted to show me. He unbuttoned his shirt and rolled it down and let me see him shaking. He was being so odd, saying and doing whatever came into his head. I didn't know what to think. Then he asked if he could listen to my heart, up close."

She shook her head again. "Isn't that the queerest thing you've ever heard?" she asked. "Has anyone ever asked to listen to your heart up close?"

Cory said no.

"I just didn't see what it would hurt, to let him," she added, staring into the car, then down at her knuckles. "To just let him lay his head down for a minute." She looked up. "But that's why I don't think Daddy should know. Ok? You know he wouldn't get it."

That said, she removed her Algebra text from the car and walked back toward the house, glancing quickly toward the road and walking, Cory thought, with a slight deliberate swing of her hips. The shed felt emptied, somehow. He slid into the car and reached into his pocket. At first he just looked at the pie, hesitant now that he knew this was the same place someone had asked to listen to his sister's heart. Where did Billy Jack get off, asking her something like that? The car still smelled like him too—his aftershave—although the smell was not so strong that it covered the stale odor of Cory's father's many years of cigarette smoking. The car was another possession Cory's father kept strict records on—mileage cost, gas and repair cost. Cory stared at the pie for awhile, then he looked up and saw his face, distorted and flat inside the rearview mirror his father always adjusted just so. He raised the pie to his mouth and began eating.

He had just finished the pie, in fact, when Billy Jack stuck his face and neck inside the tool shed and whistled at Cory through his teeth.

There was a brief moment when Cory could not have spoken if he'd wanted to. In that moment, he was sure Billy Jack had been lurking in the shadows to spy on him and had seen him eating the pie. Then Cory relaxed—this was Billy Jack, after all—and with a slight stealthy movement, barely noticeable, he dropped the pie wrapper back into his pocket and wiped his hand against his pants leg. "What are you still doing here?" Cory asked, stepping from the car. "She's gone back into the house. You'll have to go up and knock."

Billy Jack leaned his bicycle against the door and stepped fully into the tool shed. "I'm not here to see Steph," he said. He walked over to the car, red shirt still unbuttoned and hanging out of his pants, despite the night air. Cory could see the goosebumps over Billy Jack's skin, and the light in the shed was not especially strong.

"Billy Jack," he couldn't help saying. "Button up, for Christ's sake."

Billy Jack looked down at himself, jaw slack, mouth open in a circle wide as a golf ball. "It's been colder," he said. Nonetheless, he closed his shirt and buttoned it, eager to please even in a small way.

"So what do you want?" Cory asked, not wanting to move too near Billy Jack. Who was to know how sharp his eyes were, what he might see? His eyes were wide, alert, he looked at people with too much sincerity. It was unnerving. "What do you want?" Cory repeated, to hurry things along.

"I left something in your car."

"It's not my car."

"My cap," Billy Jack said. "I—left my cap in your back seat."

Cory looked down and there it was, suddenly, on the car floor, partially beneath the seat. It must have been there when he'd been sitting inside, though he hadn't noticed it. He picked the cap up and handed it to Billy Jack, who brushed strands of dirty wheat-colored hair away from his forehead before putting it on. Only he didn't give his thanks and leave like anyone would. He didn't do anything but look at his feet.

"Is there something else?" Cory asked.

"One more thing," Billy Jack said, and he even lifted his head. "You should know that nothing went on between me and Steph. I mean, nothing bad. Not like it must have looked."

"I was just kidding you," Cory said.

Billy Jack nodded. "I know," he said. "You were funny. But still. I wouldn't try to pull a fast one on her."

He was so earnest, his forehead and neck shined with sweat. Cory was embarrassed, seeing him this way, damp with openness and sincerity. They had nothing more to say to each other, but still neither of them moved. Their white breath swirled between them. Cory was doubly embarrassed, realizing this, and he tried to breathe from one side of his mouth. But Billy Jack continued breathing head-on at Cory, fog shooting in small blasts from his nose and mouth.

"Why are you telling me this?" Cory asked. "I don't care what you do, Billy Jack."

"Because you thought we were screwing around," he said. "I could tell. It was written in capitals on your face."

"Why should that worry you? That's what I don't get."

Billy Jack shrugged, like he was not so positive himself. "It wasn't true," he said again, kneeling to tie his unlaced shoe. "This is the first time I've even come over, really. I mean, into the shed and all. Steph's told me about your old man. He doesn't like you guys messing around."

Cory felt a sharpness inside his chest. He hadn't thought about the things Billy Jack might know about his life, secret private things Stephanie mumbled to him during their moments of sincerity. Cory's arms stiffened at his sides when Billy Jack stood back up.

"Usually I just sit and think about her, you know," Billy Jack said. "Don't you sit and think about things sometimes?"

There was one possible answer to that, so Cory nodded.

"Mostly I don't come over. Mostly I wait until my old man's tired out after supper, then I come out and watch your house for awhile."

"In the dark?" Cory asked.

Billy Jack looked at him, eyelids twitching. "What?"

"You watch our house in the dark?"

"There's nothing wrong with watching," he mumbled.

"How can you see a thing, if it's dark out?"

Billy Jack rubbed a small skin eruption on the side of his

forehead, just beneath his cap. "It's not so dark," he said. Then his face changed—lightened again—and he said, "I'm going there now, if you want to come and see."

"See what?"

"Where I watch your house," he said.

He meant it. He had a look in his eye. He actually tugged on Cory's jacket—the sleeve—as he passed him walking back toward the door. For one moment Cory thought of how Billy Jack could set him on edge, how you had to be careful around people so open, then his curiosity won out and he followed Billy Jack out of the shed.

By then it was almost completely dark. Billy Jack rode his bicycle across the yard, seesawing at an even pace next to Cory, and when they reached the ditch, he climbed off and began wheeling the bicycle. Together they walked into the ditch and crossed the road to the knee-high grass in the opposite ditch. They stepped into an unfenced field and began crossing at an angle. It was a small field. They stepped over old gopher holes with dirt pushed in blue mounds above the ground. The moon lifted into the sky, streaking it with weak light. Billy Jack whistled through his teeth, the way farmers did when they called in their cattle. It was a high weary sound, the only one between them. Cory kept his hands in his pockets.

They walked maybe a quarter mile when they reached a line of trees, curving into the field like the bend of an elbow. There was also a dirt path, flattened out by tractor wheels, and a few rotted-out logs. Billy Jack led him to a spot beside a large rock, some twisted brambles and a metal cylinder. Heavy with rust, the cylinder looked like it had once belonged to a tractor or large truck. Billy Jack dropped his bicycle onto the ground and walked over to Cory. Cory knew by then it was no good, he couldn't back away from Billy Jack or avoid him. Billy Jack pointed him toward the house. Two of the windows burned with light—his parents room and Stephanie's room. Cory imagined his mother was up now, awakened possibly by his father, who had come up from the basement with his ledger and pens and hidden them back inside the walnut drawer where he always kept them. He imagined Stephanie alone in her room, lying across the bed with her headset on, listening to light music but thinking of other things. It did not seem to Cory as though he was staring at the house where he lived.

"Okay, I see it," Cory mumbled. "You were right. Was that all you wanted to show me?"

"No," Billy Jack said. "Not yet." He took a small penlight from his shirt pocket and beamed it onto his wrist watch. The light globed his face with a faint pinkish ring. He looked different in that light, both more quiet and more confident. "It'll be a few," he added.

So they waited in the cool damp grass. The dew would leave a wetness when he stood, Cory thought, but this did not worry him at the moment. Billy Jack picked up the cylinder and turned it over in his hands. He didn't seem to mind how this would smudge his fingers red. When he was through he placed the cylinder between his knees and reached into his pocket for a pack of cigarettes. He lit one with a match, dragged, and handed it to Cory, who hesitated—and the thought shot directly through his head—should he put between his lips a cigarette that had been between Billy Jack's? But Cory took it, finally, and smoked too. He found he liked drawing smoke into his throat and exhaling—he liked the freedom of this.

They sat for maybe five more minutes, staring toward Cory's home and waiting. Cory had never studied his house for so long or at such a distance. He liked this distance, and the quiet of the night. The quietness itself rang in his ears. He strained to hear some sound, a dog barking or someone calling from his house. But there was nothing.

Then the yard light came on. One second he was staring at the outline of house and trees settled in darkness, the next second light spilled over the yard and through the dark trees and across the ditch, pushing out as far as the road, lighting everything like it was part of a stage show. It tossed light into the night sky and over the tool shed roof. It silver-headed the trees. The light exploded in all directions, and in a second it was over, and they could clearly see Cory's yard. Trees, hedges, the dim yellow of the house.

"I watch your light come on like that as much as I can," Billy Jack said, arms wrapped around himself, cigarette hanging between his fingers. "I know it's her turning it on, see. I can tell."

"How can you tell that?" Cory whispered, still looking over the field to his house.

"I just know it," Billy Jack said. "I feel it. She would want there to be light outside." Cory nodded, because it was true, after all, something Stephanie had always insisted on doing since they were children. She wanted to be responsible for turning on the yard light every night. "I like her doing that," Billy Jack said, lying back on his elbows and exhaling.

They both stared out some more, like it was something very special they were seeing, although it was really only Cory's house at night with the yard light on. And they were still watching when the side door opened and someone stepped from the house. "I'll bet that's your old man," Billy Jack said, squinting and lowering his voice, although they were too far off to be overhead.

Cory did look. It was very strange, seeing how small and ordinary his father looked from far off in bright lights. His father paced up the side of the house, looked around the corner and then into the trees, turned around, came back again. He sat down on the steps, lowered his face into his hands, and for one moment held them there, very still, as if he was too tired to look back up again. This was a gesture Cory would never have seen from his father if he had not been kneeling in the dark of the field, hidden from sight. Cory studied his father in this light until he'd stored the rare and fragile image firmly in his own mind. He did not know, then, how long it would have to last him.

The Shooting

T. J. held the rifle barrel-down over the kitchen table and slipped two bullets into the gun. One for the killing, the second for insurance, Laurel thought, coming up from behind. His shoulders and back were still, she saw, and erect. His hands did not tremble as he moved them. Laurel was glad for this, though she was not so lucky. Even when she held her hands together, tightly as she was now, she couldn't stop their small twitching.

Through the open window she heard their dog Randy yelping from the abandoned tool shed, each bark ending in a high-reaching whine. Since morning Randy had been howling on and off, scratching the door, jumping against the walls, chewing the wood, pawing the dirt, howling some more. She had listened to a full day of this; now it was night and cooler and Randy still howled. Often Laurel had locked herself in the bathroom, where the sound was muffled, and sat on the stool, gazing at the back yard and the grass dried brown at the tips. She'd been sitting in the bathroom, in fact, doing nothing, when T. J. came inside for a gun a couple of minutes ago. She had not been staring at the grass, though. It was night by then and too dark to see outside. Instead, she'd been staring at the circle of rust inside the tub—how had it become so thick, so red? Every week she scrubbed all the bathroom porcelain, on her knees with sponge and scratchy powders. She was not a fanatic, but she liked bathrooms that looked clean and white and smelled like plants. She could not account for the increasing stain.

"Maybe it's not such a good idea to shoot him," she said, even though she knew T. J.'s mind was already set. She wore an old loose-fitting cotton dress, turned limp from too many washings, its colors faded to the color of her own pale skin.

T. J. turned to her and lifted the gun off the table. The barrel rested against the thick of his right forearm, the gun metal a cold blue in the light. He stood so differently when he held a gun—his legs parted slightly, every muscle pulled into place— that she couldn't help staring. This is my husband, she thought at these times, and shivered. "Why?" he said. "What is it?"

"I don't know. I just thought. He's not rabid."

"He's crazy. We can't let a crazy dog run loose on the place, Laurel. You need to think."

"Of course not. I just thought—I don't know. Maybe that he'd come around." She didn't have the words or energy to explain she felt sorry for the dog that had attacked their daughter. It seemed to her a shameful feeling, one she shouldn't acknowledge aloud. Shouldn't she be angry, want vengeance, the dog's blood spilled so it could never again harm her child or anyone's children? Wasn't that what any normal mother would want? "Of course you're right," she added. "We don't have a choice."

T. J. nodded before he left the kitchen, as if they'd reached an agreement of some kind. She nodded back with a resolve she didn't feel and followed him to the screen door. He walked into the night with confidence, shoulders leaned forward, boots soft in the dirt. Once his shadow had disappeared into a line of spotted maples, she went back inside and opened a bottle of beer. It would relax her. All day she'd felt edgy, unsettled. It was more than Randy. The heat, she supposed. She rubbed the bottle along her arm until she shivered, then walked into her daughter's bedroom. It was small and dark, rather bare for a child's room—a dresser; two chairs, each seating a patchy stuffed bear; one shelf with a couple of board games and old stiff-limbed dolls bought at rummage sales. Laurel tried not to feel guilty about this, on top of everything else.

Sara was asleep on her back, one leg kicked out from under the sheet. At least she was able to sleep, Laurel thought, wondering about the exposed foot. She wanted to tuck it back inside the sheets, but she also didn't want to risk waking Sara. When Laurel looked at Sara she held her breath, as if that alone could unravel the stitches. They began above Sara's right eye, slanted at an angle across her brow, and finally disappeared into her hair line. They would leave a scar. Randy had also bitten her chest, arms, legs, but had not reached her throat. Laurel touched her own throat while thinking this, feeling inside its faint but steady pulse.

What had happened was this: she and T. J. had fought the night before Randy's attack. It had not been a special fight. It had even been mundane. She hadn't saved their grocery receipt, so T. J. couldn't check if they'd been overcharged at the grocers. "They do that sometimes," he'd said, thumping cans on the kitchen table—beans and soup and tuna marked down. Alone, she could have let his irritability pass, but he'd also scolded her, in front of Sara, for buying a small can of smoked oysters. "We really need this, don't we?" he said, sliding the can across the table. Laurel blocked it with her hands, to keep it from hurtling over the edge. "This is just the kind of spendiness that will sink us sooner or later. It's just that kind."

She glanced at Sara, kneeling on a chair with her elbows on the table, hoping, Laurel imagined, for them to remove something more than cans or dully-colored cartons from the bag. Sara may not have sensed T. J.'s accusation, but Laurel still flushed. Despite all their sensible buys—and the table was filled with them—T. J. still faulted her for the one craving she couldn't suppress, a raw hunger tucked deep inside her, beyond control. "It's not that bad," she mumbled. "A couple of dollars, is all." It might have cost more, but how could she be expected to remember exactly?

"Well. We don't seem to have a receipt or a price tag to prove that." He slumped down hard in a chair—legs spread and shoulders slumped, the posture of a rebellious school boy—and snapped on the radio. Sara walked into the living room without a word and sat in front of the TV.

"Do you want me to pay you back? Is that it?" Laurel wanted to speak louder, but Sara was still within hearing range.

"With whose money?" He glared until she turned away. The only money she had was what he gave her and they both knew it.

The next morning they still weren't talking. They used this as an excuse to sleep in and not go to church. Laurel didn't mind. Church tired her; Sunday after Sunday sitting on the hard unyielding pews, listening to lightly-accusing sermons on purity and generosity and caring with full hearts. Secretly, she felt she and T. J. possessed none of these things. They had angry secrets beneath their pressed Sunday clothes that would have flustered the pliant congregation. She preferred staying in bed for an extra hour or two and letting reality wake her gradually.

Later, while Laurel scraped together a Sunday dinner, T. J. trimmed the hedges around the house. He chopped branches decayed from too much sun, yanked obstinate leafy growth with his hands. Laurel listened to him beneath the window. She tried telling herself she needed to be more understanding. T. J. was under such pressure. The farm was not making the kind of money it once had. Despite all of this, she didn't feel as understanding as she once had. Oysters, for Christ's sake. All she'd wanted were a few minutes of special pleasure, the taste of a distant sea in her mouth. She looked through the kitchen window and saw Randy poised and still at the edge of the driveway. He stared down the gravel road, nose quivering delicately in the air. Laurel looked too but saw nothing that deserved such concentration.

At the table they ate chicken and noodles in silence. Occasionally their silver clinked against their plates and one of them would look up, startled. The fan spun in the window. Laurel imagined herself standing next to it, away from the table, face lowered, wind drawing back her hair. "Maybe you can run through the water sprinkler this afternoon," Laurel said to Sara, feeling suddenly generous. T. J. didn't respond. Laurel was disappointed, although she didn't know what she'd been hoping for. But she had been hoping for something.

"Can I bring the fat to Randy?" Sara asked, pointing at the scraps scattered across the counter. "Yes, of course," Laurel said, confused the water sprinkler idea had not caught on, embarrassed too that Sara so obviously wanted to leave the table. Maybe she sensed T. J.'s indifference? Sara picked up the greasy meat strips one by one, until she held a small fistful like a wilted bouquet. "Sara, use a napkin!" Laurel called, waving her own in the air. The screen door banged shut. Her words echoed in the still kitchen and faded without response.

111

They ignored Sara's first scream. They were used to Sara and Randy's games—Tug-o-war with a sleeve from one of T. J.'s discarded shirts, chases around the house, Sara always screaming like any normal happy child. Randy's half-growl, followed by Sara's second scream, alerted Laurel. Her heart stalled once, then pounded fast and hard, as if making up for the missed beat. "T. J.," she said, pushing her chair away, but her legs had emptied of all sensation and she could barely stand. He reached the screen door while she was still circling the table, supporting herself with the chairs. She saw his face grey as he grabbed a yardstick from a corner of the porch and ran outside, swearing under his breath. "T. J.!" she called after him.

She rushed onto the steps and paused, for a moment dizzy and confused. Outside the world was hot, too bright, and nearby something was rumbling. The car parked in the driveway reflected the sun and blinded her. She raised her hand to her eyes, blocking the glare. She saw Randy mounted across Sara, his entire body shaking as he jerked and pulled at Sara's shirt. Beneath him Sara's legs kicked. With a start, Laurel realized the dog was tearing at Sara's hair. Laurel cried out and ran down the steps. Trees and yard twisted around her. T. J. hit Randy on the back with the yardstick, so hard the dry crack made Laurel cringe and the animal jump away, like a rabbit hopping backward. The air was heavy and dense and she felt it pressing into her lungs. T. J. yelled and with an effort she tried to hear him, thinking he was shouting her instructions. "Goddamn it!" he yelled. "Goddamn." He bent over, scooping Sara into the bend of his arm. Panting, Randy moved toward them and T. J. kicked him squarely between the ribs. Laurel heard the impact—boot into soft belly, the outward rush of air. The dog's legs buckled and it sank onto the gravel. "Oh," Laurel said, still clutching the napkin in her hand.

She picked up a screaming Sara and sat on the lawn with her. Laurel wasn't thinking clearly. She was shaking so, and Sara was screaming. "Get inside!" T. J. yelled and Laurel stared at him for a moment, not understanding. He looked so distant, standing inside a wave of heat, a greasy sky behind him—and all this beyond her reach.

Finally Laurel understood and carried Sara into the house. Her confusion was replaced by terror—at Sara's crying, at the blood running down her face, at the clog of dog spit stuck like gum in her hair. She sat Sara on the bathroom stool, wet a rag and wiped it across the girl's face. As soon as Laurel cleaned the bite, more blood would fill it. "It's okay, it's okay," she whispered, lowering the rag and wiping blood and gravel from Sara's arms and legs, then bringing it back to the girl's forehead, which bled still. The rag grew soft and fragile with blood. "Sara, lift your arms," Laurel said. She stared at her daughter's blood slipping through her fingers and terror rose in her, coloring her face and slowing her words. Maybe it was terror or maybe it was something more. "Lift your arms so I can take off your shirt. Hurry now."

Sara obeyed. Laurel tugged the ripped T-shirt over Sara's head and saw the marks of Randy's teeth circling the right side of her chest—deep purple indentations with a white ridge of skin around each. "It's not so bad," Laurel lied, trying not to grimace as she rinsed the rag, squeezing blood into the sink's drain.

They both flinched when something hit the kitchen wall. Something's fallen, Laurel thought, though the sound was louder, too jarring for this. T. J.'s yell was followed by a second crash. Sara stopped crying, her eyes wide. "He's mad," she mumbled and covered herself with her bruised arms. It was an adult gesture, simple and protective; Laurel couldn't bear to see

113

this, she understood the gesture so well.

"No he's not, honey," Laurel said. "At least not at you." She pressed the cleaned rag once more against Sara's temple. "Hold this. Tight." When Laurel stood, she leaned against the wall for a moment because her vision had gone dark. She could see only shapes, outlines, her life a blur. She reached for the door knob and, when her vision cleared, saw how white her hand looked holding the dirty gold knob.

She hurried into the kitchen, saw T. J. pick up a chair with both hands, then toss it sideways—like a discus—high against the wall toward the wall's heavy mounted wood clock. His muscle T-shirt was dark with sweat and looked slippery against his back. She wanted to scream for him to stop, but how would that sound, her own loud words mixed in the air with his? How would that sound to Sara? She swallowed instead. "T. J., stop it," she whispered. When he didn't seem to hear, she stepped farther into the kitchen. A chair slammed against the side of the stove and bounced twice on the floor, as if it had been dribbled. The stove burner lids hopped into the air. "Stop it," she said again. "You're scaring Sara."

When he turned to her, his nose running like a baby's, she thought he was going to hit her. Then she thought he would start crying. She wasn't sure which frightened her more. She had to hold onto him. It was the only thing. "Take it easy," she said, her fingers clutching him before he pulled away; in that moment, she felt him shiver. He looked so hot, but his skin beneath the sweaty flush was cold. She couldn't think of what to say. She had never seen T. J. like this—without some reserve.

"Is she all right?" he asked finally, feeling his way down into the nearest chair.

"We've got to bring her to a doctor," Laurel said.

114

His shoulders trembled then, too, as he stared up at her, his head cocked. His right foot was twisted to one side, so severely Laurel thought the shoe would split down the middle.

"T. J.," she whispered, without thinking, "she's bleeding. Randy might be rabid."

"Rabies?" T. J. repeated the word twice more before his eyes showed some understanding. "We can't afford a doctor," he said. "Rabies shots take weeks, isn't that right?"

"We can't think about that now. T. J? We have no choice. She's been bitten in the head." Laurel tapped her own temple. "Please, T. J., it's her head."

For several seconds he stared at his hands gripping his knees. He turned his hands up—the flats red and creased, a blister near the thumb. His nails were very short, crusted beneath the cuticles, and one nail was black. "Get her ready," he said flatly, standing up. "I'll be back in a few minutes."

She noticed the hard shine in his eyes but didn't dare ask him where he was going. She ran back to the bathroom, ignoring the pulse of pain in her chest. "It's all right, Daddy's just worried about you," she said and carried Sara to the bedroom. Sara had stopped crying but seemed dulled somehow. When Laurel sat her on the bed Sara did not look up, only gazed straight ahead, eyes unfocused like she'd opened them to an unexpectedly bright morning. Was this shock then? She helped Sara change clothes, keeping the child's back to the window. From it Laurel could see T. J. with a pitchfork in his hands, holding it out, backing Randy into the open tool shed—and Randy trying to circle him enough to break free. She did not want Sara to see her father and pet brought to this—outside facing off in the heat and slanted sun, each move slow and calculated.

115

Laurel swallowed more beer. It was unbearable, rethinking these things. Sara continued to sleep, undisturbed. In the end, Randy had not been rabid—the sheriff and two specialists had driven out yesterday to confirm this—which still left Laurel and T. J. with a mad dog in their tool shed. Early this morning the sheriff had returned alone with an offer to shoot Randy, but T. J. had said he would do it, in a firm decisive voice that stilled her protest before it had formed into words.

Now Randy stopped barking suddenly, as if a hand had closed around his throat. Laurel lifted her head, staring at the window, the dark glass. "T. J. just opened the door," she whispered aloud and closed her eyes.

But she didn't hear a gun shot.

After a few seconds she reopened her eyes, confused. Maybe T. J. was taking his time aiming. She left Sara's room and sat at the kitchen table with the beer, straining now to hear the shot. She stroked the sides of the bottle, pushed her hair from her eyes. She would never understand what had happened to Randy. He'd been such a gentle dog; anyone exposed to him for even a few minutes said as much. She remembered those moments when Randy would run with Sara, around and around the house until, exhausted, he would lie in the grass and Sara, impatient, would tug his ears until he stood again. Often Sara had fallen asleep in the yard with her head pillowed against Randy's stomach, giving Laurel time to concentrate on other work without worrying about Sara. She'd come to think of Randy as an ally, in spite of an occasional nagging guilt that Randy took better care of Sara than either she or T. J.

And now this.

Still Laurel heard nothing. She couldn't wait any longer. Another minute and she would leap to her feet, start pacing, peer through curtains. She placed the bottle back in the refrigerator

116

and walked outside. Sara was asleep and she would only be gone a few minutes. She had to know what was happening.

The night was hot, and so dry she smelled it in the odor of the dying cornfields. Trees stood languid and still. Even the moon plastered in the sky seemed hot, sluggish. As Laurel walked, mosquitoes stung her arms, her legs, though she couldn't see them in the darkness. She ignored the bugs. She had walked across the lawn and was nearing the tool shed before it occurred to her, dimly, that something might be wrong with T. J.

She squinted until she saw the tool shed, on a bare grassless rump of ground. The door was open. T. J. stood barely inside, beneath the unshaded bulb, his gun lowered to one side. The light threw his shadow large against the shed. She stared at him, uncertain now. "T. J.?" she mumbled, so she would not startle him.

He didn't turn to her, only rubbed his face with his free hand. She walked up behind him, softly, so she could see over his shoulder. The shed was empty except for a dusty sack of feed slumped on the floor, two rusted shark-tooth saws hanging from nails, and a stack of empty paint cans in the nearest corner. Randy had backed into the far corner, where the light was weakest. Despite these shadows, his eyes were twin circles of light that betrayed him, giving T. J. a clear shot. Laurel felt she could have shot Randy, effortlessly, from that distance.

"What is it?" she asked. At the sound of her voice, Randy growled but didn't move. She felt cold, staring inside at what was once their pet, now wild and cautious and crouched in shadow.

"Don't come in," T. J. said, back still turned.

"I won't. Why haven't you shot him?"

Because of the dim light, she could see only one side of T. J.'s

117

face—his cheek and neck pale, all his visible skin a clean and startling white. Maybe it was the light. He was staring at Randy, and Laurel was sure Randy, crouched in the corner, stared back. Only now Randy was effectively cornered and contained and they were all caught in a moment of waiting.

"You said you'd shoot him," she reminded T. J.

"You said we shouldn't." They were both quiet. Still T. J. didn't raise the gun. Laurel did not move or bend to slap mosquitoes from her knees, afraid of the reaction an unexpected move might have on Randy or, worse, T. J.

"Goddamn dog," T. J. mumbled, shaking his head. His shoulders had started shaking, and she knew from experience the trembling would soon spread to his arms and hands. She remembered when T. J., after cornering and locking Randy inside the tool shed, had come back inside and driven her and Sara to the doctor. He had been shaking then too, his hands unsteady on the steering wheel. He'd been shivering, really, since Randy's attack. This was half of what frightened her so much. This and her own pity and compassion for the dog growing so strong inside her she could barely feel anything else.

"Please, shoot him." Laurel didn't recognize her own voice—kind yet firm and sure.

T. J. shifted his feet in the dirt dried to a fine yellow dust. Laurel said again, in a whisper somehow louder than her last remark. "Shoot him. Get it over with."

Randy stirred in the corner then. T. J. lifted the gun, positioned it against his shoulder, aimed with a deliberate concentration, and fired without flinching. Laurel winced but did not close her eyes. The blast echoed through the shed, vibrating the air inside and then outside, rattling the night for a couple fleeting seconds, then all was quiet. Randy collapsed without a whine, the points of light merely sinking lower to the ground and finally rolling up as Randy's head dropped to one side. Laurel backed away and leaned against the door, releasing breath slowly from her chest until she felt emptied and light.

T. J. lowered the rifle but remained standing in the same position. His back was still turned away, so she couldn't see if shooting Randy had stopped the shaking from moving to his hands and face. If she could have predicted what he would do after he turned around, maybe she wouldn't have needed to see.

He remained motionless for a few more seconds, then he stepped inside the shed. Laurel watched as he walked over to Randy, kneeled down, lay the gun in the dirt. She felt a moment's panic, seeing T. J. unarmed and thinking, unreasonably, that Randy was not yet dead, that he could still attack them somehow. Then T. J. reached down and ran his hand over Randy's still undamaged fur. He did this several times, then lifted the dog like it was a baby, the neck curved over his arm. Laurel watched this tenderness from T. J., so long in coming, and could not speak.

"We could bury him tomorrow," Laurel whispered when T. J. passed her, carrying the dog toward the field beyond the shed. But he shook his head. "I'll do it now," he said. From somewhere Laurel thought she heard crying—a child's distant call— then realized with a start it was Sara, now awake and alone inside the house. Laurel hurried back through the hot night, feeling stronger and more confident than she had a right to, and once she'd soothed Sara back to sleep, she waited for T. J. to come back from the shadows where he'd buried Randy. He did come back, though Laurel was almost asleep when he entered their bedroom, his shoulders bowed, and removed his T-shirt speckled with Randy's blood.

Out of Body

I'd been driving since early morning, but it was late cold afternoon before I turned a bend in the road and saw the barn.

I pulled to the side and killed the engine. It was because of a catch in my chest, sharp like pain can get. So I took a pack of menthols from the glove compartment and lit a cigarette. I smoked through that catch. In my mind, the barn had been larger. I was a half mile drive away, but still. I was disappointed, in a small way not worth mentioning.

For awhile I sat inside the car—hunched in my coat, heat blasting—and squinted through the smudged windshield across the bared-clean fields. The farm house had been repainted, but the barn looked the same. Except smaller. I didn't know what to make of that. I cranked up the heater. Late autumn wind can be unremitting, the way it rises over hills, pushes across prairies, shivers around houses, steals under doors and poorly-caulked windows. What can you do about it? You can insulate, but that's the problem with insulation. It's never one hundred percent.

There are always cracks you can't find or don't know about. The cold alone finds them.

I lit a second cigarette with the smoldering butt of my first. I wasn't ready to drive that final half mile, not yet. The barn scared me, really. I can admit that. Once I was this scrawny fifteen year old farm kid with a cheap set of binoculars and a thing about bats. The barn loft, high and dark, drew them in. One twilight, binoculars in hand, I climbed into the loft, it stinking of bird and animal shit. I walked to the loft's edge, where there was nothing around but space for bats to fly. I looked across, then up, at the spread of air. I didn't look down. Twine snared my feet, I turned to shake them loose, and then I was falling, back first, straight toward my father's tractor disk below. The disk was a gravity pulling me down. It wanted me, I could feel that. Only I couldn't see the disk. Two bats wing-fluttering through the rafters was all I saw in my spin through space.

I landed in the hay between two blades. When I hit, the binoculars snapped from my neck and shattered against the nearest blade. But I was uninjured. Night after night, I paid this debt back in dreams. I walked into my room and found the disk where my bed used to be. Or, in the backyard, my father was driving a tractor, digging furrows for some huge garden. Then he drove through the house, knocking down walls and running over furniture—dressers, sofa, TV set—but he missed my room where I stood on the bed, watching. When he drove close he pulled me onto the seat and let me steer. I dreamed of falling, of stepping on nails, of watching animals gather at the barn door, skin falling away from their bones. And in early morning, when my sheets were dark with sweat and I thought there was no dreaming possibly left in me, I'd dream once more. I lay in a hard bed while my mother, a gentle woman, unwrapped bandages from my body. She stood, backed off trem-

124

bling, dropped the bandages from her hands. But I couldn't see what she did.

There are other reasons for staying awake nights, of course. Too much caffeine and chain smoking. Too many catches in the chest or the small of the back. Too many girlfriends who phone late, voices slurred from drink or loneliness or both, wondering why they're alone in their apartments and I'm alone in mine and all the bars have closed. And too many worries about my health, my weak and irregular heart, though I'm only thirty and shouldn't have to worry about such things. Eventually it all leads back to the barn. It's like I lost something there.

Although I hadn't noticed at first, I'd parked in front of the house where old Mrs. Terrell used to live. I was maybe twenty feet from the mailbox, which advertised a new name. Sholer. I recognized that name, in an indifferent way. A Sholer family had lived in town near the Lutheran church once, when I was a boy. The Sholer's new yard was large and well-mowed and featured several pink plastic flamingos, all balanced on one leg, each of their open mouths a shallow bath for sparrows and other small summer birds. When Mrs. Terrell lived here, the grass had sprung knee-high, making good shade for field mice and flat-bellied snakes.

One day in church, after hearing about my fall, Mrs. Terrell had slipped her offering into my shirt pocket. She leaned close, smelling of old olives, church perfume, Polygrip. She crouched down, secretively, her bones sounding. She wore yellow polyester, a loose dangle of beads. It was a hot day, sure, but her hands on me were cold. "You're a lucky boy," she said, mouthing the words so I barely heard, one hand trembling around my elbow, the other twisting and untwisting her beads. Later, at home and alone, I opened the envelope and two with-

125

ered dollar bills drifted into my lap. They smelled like her and the deep insides of her purse. I hid these plus envelope under a loose patch of carpet at the foot of my bed. I felt like I'd stolen the money.

"Most of us do not have the kind of luck you're in for," she'd said, twice, before she let go of my elbow.

A week later, she fell from a stool, broke a hip, and died before the UPS man knocked on her door with a package. The man peered through the window, my father explained, who knew him—the man peered through and saw her lying on the floor, winking shards of broken jar around her, purple jam spotting her dress and white arms. If she hadn't died, she would have been paralyzed. That was my father's opinion. She was an old woman, after all. Then he walked into the bathroom and stared out the screen window toward the barn, at the sun dipping behind its silver dome. I never dared salvage the two dollars after that. They may still be under that patch of carpet.

I was about finished with cigarette number two when I saw a girl in sweat pants and a long sleeved shirt with hood jogging around the curve in the road. I wiped the window with my fist. I saw her before she saw me. She ran with her eyes fixed on the road, breath released harsh and hard into the air. Then she saw the car and stopped, stared for a moment. "Hey!" she called.

Of course she was talking to me. I was the only one sitting inside a car parked in front of someone's house. I stepped out, feeling unsure, my boots crunching the gravel. It was a strangely comforting sound. "Hello," I said, waving my cigarette hand at her.

She stared toward me. Once, briefly, she paused, glancing toward the white-curtained house, then shook her head and continued toward me, calling "hey" once more and shielding her eyes with one hand, the way she would if she was looking into the sun. Her hair was a thick long-reaching braid down the center of her back. The letters on the front of her sweats spelled BPHS.

"What are you doing out here?" she asked. She stood many feet away, keeping a distance between us. I respected that caution. "Do you want something?" she added.

I sat on the car hood. She was familiar to me, in a way I couldn't place. It wasn't the way she looked, really, just some presence about her. "The car's resting," I said. "Are we bothering you?"

Her brows raised, like she hadn't expected me to quiz. "I live here," she said, nodding at the house. "With my mother," she added like someone had asked. I nodded back, because I had nothing to say, but by then I'd made the connection between this girl and the Mrs. Sholer who had once lived in town. The summer I fell and Mrs. Terrell died was also the summer Mrs. Charles Sholer was pregnant. Every Sunday she would slip into church alone and sit in the back beneath one of two stained glass windows—an odd Jesus with wings holding a lamb, or a normal Jesus feeding bread to bearded men who gazed at him inquisitively and with longing. Every Sunday she left before the service was finished, hand to her mouth or stomach or waving a church bulletin in front of her face. She was married then but I never once saw her husband in church. A couple of years later, he walked out on her and his little girl, Monica. Monica Sholer.

I remember one time. Mrs. Sholer came to church late and slipped into the pew beside me. This was after Monica had been born. Mrs. Sholer held the baby Monica slanted into her chest; I was uncomfortable, seeing this. The baby was so small, feet the size of matchbox cars, toes kicking inside pink socks that would have fit my father's thumbs. I think it was the first time I'd been close to anything so tiny and also human. I didn't want to ex-

127

hale in their direction. I was afraid my breath would smell.

Now the teen Monica wiped her brow and watched me until her breath had quieted. It was clear she didn't recognize me. There was no reason she should, really. The last time I'd been inside that church, Monica had been six or maybe seven. My fall had occurred before her time. I was before her time. "My mother doesn't like to mess with strangers, is all," she said. "I'm sure she knows you're out here. Are you selling something?"

"Not at all," I said. "I'm resting." I couldn't resist staring toward the house, though, because I pictured Mrs. Sholer staring out through the trim lace curtains, a spinster now, hair graying, skin flaking, some high carbo supper for her athlete daughter bubbling forgotten over the stove's gas burners. For one second I wanted to point or make a face. I wanted to do whatever would cause her to look close and remember who I was. But I also felt bad for her inside, afraid of me outside.

"I thought the car was resting," Monica said.

"Of course. Him, too. Actually, we're a team. Whatever he does, I do, too."

"You never know what to think these days, is all. You could be someone weird. How would we know?"

The cigarette was a burned-down nub between my fingers, but I was suddenly reluctant to flick it into the gravel. The truth was, I did feel weird—strange and secretive—for knowing who she was when she hadn't a clue about me. "Why are you running on a day like this?" I asked, to change the subject.

"Regionals next week." She bent down and touched her knees with her elbows a few times. Then, straightening, she unzipped her sweat top and shook her arms free. She was a strong girl, I saw, but thin, her arms dropping long and ropey with muscle from her T-shirt. I could see her sweat. "Jesus, that looks cold," I said.

She gazed over at me, holding her rolled sweat top close. "That's just it," she said. "I've been running."

A minute passed. Then two. I tossed the cigarette butt aside, finally, and lit another, my third. I felt no guilt. My doctors weren't always patient with my smoking, how I wouldn't cut back despite the catches and murmurs and accelerated heart beats, but they were hundreds of miles away now, barely a thought.

"Well?" Monica said.

I lay flat on the hood, knees up, arms stretched across the windshield. The hood was still warm in one spot, so I centered myself and lowered the curve of my back into it. I did this partly because my back had cramped, partly because of the weird silence between us.

Partly because it was the only thing that came to mind, and I felt the need to do something.

Monica walked closer, with me supine and all. I suppose she was getting used to me. "So what do you want? I've got to tell Momma something. You're not just going to sleep, are you?"

When you're down and looking up, it's hard to judge distance. The sky looks nearer, somehow, though just as cold and gray and impersonal. "I used to live around here," I said. "Right over there."

And I pointed to the barn where my father, finding me winded between the disk blades, kneeled and whispered my name.

"Really?" she said without interest.

"You bet. I almost died there."

That always gets people. I felt her shrinking back, though I couldn't see this clearly. I told her about my fall and imagined her change in expression: brows raised, jaw dropped, mouth O-ed. Death by machinery is nothing to scoff at in the sticks.

"At the Duncan's?" she asked finally, arms folded around herself.

"Yes. Although then, it wasn't the Duncan's. The barn belonged to my father. The whole farm did. It was the Mitchell's."

"That's where you're going?" she asked. "To the Duncan's?"

"To the barn. Yes. As long as I'm here. Just to drive by, I mean. Not to go inside."

But I didn't get up. Instead I shifted my jacket—raised it a little—so I could feel the fading heat through my shirt. The shirt had belonged to my father once, if that mattered. He and my mother had moved to Texas a couple years ago, where they could live the remainder of their days without worry in the sun. Naturally I haven't written them about my health.

"What are you doing now?" Monica asked, impatient.

"The engine's still warm."

"It can't be that warm," she said. "It's not going to stay warm for long."

I didn't answer. I was thinking of winters past, when I was about Monica's age, and would sneak to the barn some nights. I would sit on the stump and wait for myself to grow very cold. It was a game. How long could I stand it? First I would remove my gloves and rest my hands on one stationary knee, watching them purple. Then I would lift my bony, stiff-knuckled fingers to my face, smiling at how thick they felt, how slow they moved in front of me. Finally I would take off my parka. The barn cats gazed out from between hay bales, and occasionally one or two walked over to huddle in the warmth of my feet. I resisted drop-

130

ping my hands into their fur. I stayed in the barn, just like that, until I felt the cold inside me instead of just around me. Until I felt it like a fist closing inside my chest. Then, legs shaking, boots heavy around my feet, I'd throw on my coat and stagger from the barn into the too white world of snow and ice-heavy trees tilting around me. The more I ran, the more strong and sure my legs became. My booted feet felt lighter. The blood inside me surged, heating up, spreading outward to chest, arms, legs. I felt all of this. I always knew I would make it back to the house. But that happened before I fell.

Meanwhile, the cigarette was fizzing away to nothing between my fingers. I inhaled, breathing a moment of life back into it.

"I've had it," Monica said. "Go drive by, if that's what you're going to do. I'm going back inside."

"In a minute. I'm smoking. Don't let me keep you, Monica."

I didn't even think about what I'd said. I had been thinking her name in my mind the whole while anyway. But, hearing her name, she moved closer, though not so close that I could see her clearly without turning my head. "Where did you get my name?" she asked.

I realized my mistake then, of course, but it was too late. I shrugged.

"You said my name," she said. "I don't know you."

I turned to her, feeling an opportunity of some kind, a desire, though I could not explain what that was. "I knew you once. When I lived here. You were very small. You wouldn't remember."

She stared at me, waiting for more, because my face was flushing and I was filling with a need to talk, to explain something, and she must have noticed this. "But it's not really like

131

I'm a stranger," I continued. "You see? Because I knew you. You don't have to wonder about me. I'm only going to see where I used to live." I felt my heart rattling inside my chest, from the possibilities I sensed briefly in that moment. In that moment, I thought I might ask her to go with me to the Duncan's. She knew them, she could explain my case, they would give me permission to actually walk inside the barn where it had all begun. But then I regained sense and I could not ask such a thing. I didn't know her, not really. I lay back down on the hood.

The chill was rising around us. And the dark. I wouldn't be able to see the goddamned barn soon, but I stayed down. I felt like you do after you've been gassed in a dentist's chair—thick and fuzzy and not quite yourself. Now the heat had disappeared at my spine, so I was lying only on plain cold metal. I didn't care. At that moment, in that position, I didn't care about a lot. The barn seemed too much an effort to get to, suddenly, even at this close range. So what if I'd driven myself across a full state to get there? What was the purpose of any of it? The cigarette I held burned down toward my fingers.

Finally Monica stomped over, so she was looking straight down at me. I saw her face clearly for the first time—green eyes flashing, braid hanging over one shoulder, hands reaching down toward me. She snatched the cigarette butt from my fingers and ground it to dust under one sneakered heel.

"You can't stay here. Would you get up and move?" She put her hand on my shoulder and shook me. I felt myself, slowly, shiver.

I waited until she'd gone back inside, then I stood up. In the end, I knew I had to see the trip through. I would drive to my old house alone, turn into the driveway, stare for several unwavering seconds, car headlights gleaming. Maybe inside the house, the Duncans would look out their windows, wondering about company, or glance up from their kitchen table at the glare. A child would point at the light spilling across the ceiling. I would stare at the barn and the house and, maybe, too, the faces of the Duncans against the windows, staring out at me, a part of their past they had never known. I would stare until I was satisfied, then drive off the way I'd come, back toward my present life.

First, though, I stood at the car in the wind. I unzipped my coat and held it open. The wind was not especially strong, but it was enough to snap at my shirt and slip inside the empty spaces between buttons. I opened my mouth, sucked in the sharp air, filled my lungs with it. I imagined the air were cold hands—many hands—against my chest, massaging my heart, lifting all pain from me one last time.

Harvest

Two years before Uncle Norm's visit, when Pam was fourteen and I was twelve, she woke one morning and couldn't step out of bed. It was her spine, turned to lead overnight. "Help, is anyone there?" she had called, pounding a weak fist against the wall. Downstairs, my parents and I glanced up from our breakfasts and crusty morning thoughts. The moment before she called, I was staring into my glass of juice, at the orange pulp stuck along its sides.

Pam had viral meningitis then and spent a couple weeks in a private hospital room, breathing only germ-free air. One wrong virus, her doctors warned, stethoscopes hanging from their necks—one wrong virus could paralyze her or worse. For that week, we weren't allowed to touch her. Inside her room we wore face masks and disposable plastic gloves, for our own protection as well. Meningitis was contagious. "Hello, baby girl, can you say hi to us?" our mother would ask, stroking the metal bedpost, mouth twisted behind her mask. But Pam rarely answered or glanced up, just lay still and breathed pure air—chest rising, falling back, eyes so tightly closed they seemed glued. Occasionally nurses drifted in to poke silver needles into her arms. I watched from a chair beside the window, feeling distant from them and the doctors in the hall, forever explaining new tests and complications to my parents. Sometimes I would stare at my fingers through the gloves, imagining the millions of germs there I couldn't see.

During Pam's worst time, my father began making phone calls. At night, after the two of us had returned from the hospital, he spent hours whispering on the phone, back turned away. Miserable, I listened anyway, catching what fragments I could: "monitored" and "a kind of quarantine," "she can't be moved" and "it's not even Pam, it's Irene." One night, after he'd hung up, he kneeled beside me, close, his dry breath in my face. I flinched and turned away, embarrassed. "Your mother and I have agreed to let your Uncle Norm stay with you for awhile," he said. "He wants to help, however he can. That way I can be at the hospital with your mother and sister until we get the All Clear. You want that, don't you?"

I had only one solid memory of Uncle Norm. Clean-shaven, hair slicked back with Brylcream, he had twirled a spatula beside our hissing outdoor grill and paid me a nickel for each of my five-second handstands. I knew there must be other times I'd seen him, long ago, but I couldn't remember or imagine them, so they didn't seem real. I thought only of that handful of nickels I had sealed in a jar and placed in the windowsill, and how they collectively heated in the summer sun. If I removed one from the jar in afternoon, it burned in my hand.

I told my father yes, I wanted that.

The day my father drove to the bus terminal to meet Norm, my mother sat with me in the hospital hallway outside Pam's

138

room, drinking Orangeade from a can. "This will only be for a little while, honey, and your Uncle Norm will be fine, he's a little eccentric, but there are worse things." She was about to tell me a story about Uncle Norm, in fact, when my father rounded the corner, alone. "Must have missed the bus," he mumbled. Head bowed, he put on his mask and plastic gloves, then leaned against the hospital door before stepping into Pam's room. My mother watched as the heavy door closed behind him, one slow inch at a time. Then she squeezed the can by its middle and tossed it at the small wastebasket nearby. Although she missed, she didn't stand to pick the can up. Orange drink leaked into the middle of the corridor, but not even the nurses passing by bothered to mop the puddle up. They stepped over it and continued on their way.

Uncle Norm never did come. Later that week, sun white across her bed, Pam began to improve and no one mentioned Uncle Norm again.

I was nearing fifteen the summer he came uninvited into our house, a bony and gaunt man shivering inside his clothes. He had a long creased face and his hair was just beginning to grey at the roots. His hands and arms were pale, almost white, beneath their dark growth of hair. His glasses, deeply scratched, fit him loosely, like he'd picked them up off a street corner. None of these things explained Pam's and my instant attraction to him. Maybe it was his eyes, behind those glasses looking hard at us, sometimes into us, in a way our parents rarely looked. In those days they were like shadows passing in the halls. They smiled at us the way they would people in church they recognized but couldn't place. Or maybe it was the way Uncle Norm talked, sometimes telling stories until our heads nodded to one side. His voice drew us in.

Originally, our father said Uncle Norm would stay only a day or two, until he was feeling better. That day or two became three, then four. By the fourth night, our mother was restless. After supper she asked our father if she could please speak to him. He exhaled, rolled his eyes, and whispered for Pam and I to leave the room because our mother wanted a Discussion. He lifted his brows, so we would see what torture she put him through, all of which he tolerated, of course, for our benefit.

Upstairs I played Solitaire on Pam's bed while she polished her toenails the color of plums. I also removed from my pocket an old pipe of my father's—still tasting lightly of tobacco—and popped it into my mouth. We listened to our parents through the thin floor and watched the moths and deer flies flicking against the window screen.

Normally during Discussion, our mother would talk while our father mumbled, "right, right," and knuckle-drummed the table top. Often she wanted to Discuss how the family should go out more, to a restaurant or the movies. Wouldn't he enjoy taking his wife and two bright children into town for a feature? All we'd have to do was sit inside the dark theatre and watch the latest blockbuster with popcorn cups balanced on our legs. "Right," our father would answer, "except pay, of course. You forgot that little detail."

That always shut her up, because the factory where he worked was never doing well. But upstairs, Pam would get dreamy-eyed whenever movies were mentioned. Pam was a movie buff. Every week she hoarded her lunch money and waited for our monthly trips into town for garage sales, where she would buy grocery bags fat with used movie magazines. She read each one cover to cover, lingering on the photos of famous couples clinching in front of their serene blue pools. She stacked old issues on her book shelf except for two, which held up the uneven back leg of her bed.

But this particular night, our mother didn't talk movies. Uncle Norm concerned her more. How long was he planning to hostel in our basement? He'd been there four days and nights and she'd begun to feel foolish, walking only so far into her own cellar and asking Norm to please hand her a can of fruit from the shelf over his head. What did he do down there all day? That he chose to remain downstairs, with poor lighting and the old sofa, worried her.

"Quiet," our father said. "He might hear." Where else would Norm go, when he had no other close family and trouble keeping his feet on the ground?

As it turned out, the feet on the ground part was almost literal. According to our father, Uncle Norm had started hitching down to visit us but passed out kneeling in the bathroom of the first small town bar he came across, his head under a sink's running tap. A kindly bartender shook him back to consciousness, then phoned the cops, who in turn called our father, who had no choice but to bring Norm back here. "I was going to surprise you, Tom, is all," Uncle Norm had said. "To see how the girl's doing these days. How all of you are doing. I didn't plan to be doing so poorly myself."

Now Pam whispered, "These discussions have gone terminal," and, on her heels, walked into the hall, inching along the wall toward the laundry chute. When we were younger, Pam and I had used the chute as a phone. I would lay my face against the cool heap of dirty laundry and stare up at her broad white face peering down, voice sounding like metal. "Uncle Norm," Pam whispered now into the chute. "Earth to Uncle Norm."

141

He took a few seconds, but finally up came his voice. "Nice of you to call, Earth," he said.

"How's the basement?"

"It sure could use a beer."

"We'll be down after they go to bed." Pam closed the chute and, back in the room, started on her other foot. There was a time she'd let me do a toenail, if I asked. I'd lift her foot into my lap and try not to paint outside the lines.

We waited until our parents had gone to bed and the house sounded empty and still, then snuck downstairs. The night stretched before us, rich with possibility. First we nabbed two slender-necked bottles of our father's beer from the refrigerator. Two he wouldn't miss, so Pam decided to be daring and take three. "Are you kidding?" I asked. She told me to grow up and find some backbone. The extra we could share.

In the basement Uncle Norm was stretched across the sofa, our mother's quilt around his arms and knees. He pulled at loose threads and twisted them around his knuckles. "Thanks," Uncle Norm said. "I could be down and kicking before I'd expect a sip from those two upstairs."

While we talked, Pam and I passed a bottle between us. There was something good about sitting with Pam in the dark on our mother's braided rug, drinking beer and listening to Uncle Norm talk about the city. "The basement wouldn't seem so shabby to your parents if they'd lived where I have," he said. Uncle Norm had lived in a YMCA, once, sweeping floors and cleaning bathrooms in exchange for a free room. "Didn't matter, though," he said. "The cleaning. You can't clean a Y. All those men drifting in and out, who knows what they're carrying? You kids would smell it in the air, all that shabbiness. This basement's more like a California suite."

Eventually he got around to talking about movies. In the city,

142

he could see them whenever he wanted, with a little pocket change, and the one thing he liked as much as a good drink was a good movie. He believed he'd been a projectionist in a former life, back when movies were silent and jerky on the screen. Then he'd seen as many movies as he pleased, suspended mid-air in a tiny booth throwing light against the walls, and he'd drunk as much as he liked too. Ushers in stiff uniforms never beamed flashlights into his face and told him to take it outside, because he was the management.

In this life, Uncle Norm's favorite theatre was named the Palace. Every night its lights winked on and off. The lobby was like a castle's entrance—marble floors, mirrors hung on walls, deep red rugs that led you into darkness. The man or woman who tore your ticket looked you in the eye with respect, as if you were sharing some secret. They smiled and showed their teeth.

"There's one movie I saw that's still in my head," he whispered. This movie concerned an orb of space sirens that landed in a cornfield outside small town America. "These ladies had the *hair*," Uncle Norm said. "Like beehives, and their skin was silver. Their lips were blue." When they opened their mouths, haunting melodies drifted through the air. In town, men looked up from their newspapers and TV sets. They abandoned their cars in the streets. All zombie-walked toward the field, arms open, reaching for what lay beyond the stalks. In this way the men were gathered, and once stored in beams of light, the sirens wiggled around an arms-crossed mummy lying inside a glass coffin. Eyes falling open, moaning, he rose up, peeled the bandages from his skin, gulped his first earth air. The sirens kneeled to him, chanted, "Commandor! Commandor!" Uncle Norm remembered how the Commandor lumbered through the streets for the blood of the town's unprotected women, a cold greedy spark firing his eyes. Fortunately, the strongest and

143

handsomest man in town was also deaf in one ear. The sirens call rang dimmer, confusing him. Should he follow, should he fight? He debated this while the Commandor peeked through windows, hid between the dresses in women's closets. In time the young hero snapped to and set a trap with the help of the town's prettiest ingenue—also, luckily, a gifted organist. The next night she played church hymns on her home organ, so movingly the Commandor couldn't resist following her music. He wandered up the girl's long driveway, climbed the pipes to her bedroom, where he would hide in her closet, yes, wait for her to sleep, so he could lower his mouth over her neck and drink. Instead, he found the young man waiting for him with fists clenched. They grappled in front of the bedroom window, then the Commandor was tossed, through splintering glass and night air, to the swimming pool below. He belly-hit the water and, heavy from listless small town blood, sank to the bottom. Their plans for conquest dashed, the sirens sprang the men from the beams and orb-flew back to their home planet while the credits rolled.

"I saw that mother twice," Uncle Norm said. "It had that special quality that makes you want to see a movie over and over."

When I asked what that quality was, he squinted at me like I meant to be smart. "It's not a quality you *define*," he said. "It's the kind you *feel*. Deep inside yourself." Pam said she understood, certainly, but could only speak for herself. I felt bad, her saying she'd only speak for herself, but I stayed quiet. I bit my pipe instead and imagined sirens outside our house, darting across the roof or through untrimmed brush under my window, calling for me in voices high and forlorn.

A week into Uncle Norm's visit, our father decided Pam and I should dig potatoes from the garden. Just turned September,

144

school starting soon: it was time. Our mother suggested that if Uncle Norm planned to live indefinitely in our basement, shouldn't he get a shovel, too?

That was how, after a week of bunking in our basement, Uncle Norm ended up under the hot sun with Pam and me. He wore dark sunglasses, baggy pants, a ripped T-shirt, and for shade, our mother's wide-rimmed straw hat. He followed us into the garden our first day, stepping into our footprints like he didn't trust the dirt. For most of the morning I dug, Pam wiped the potatoes clean and stacked them, and Uncle Norm crouched beside us to Supervise. "Every good operation needs an Overseer," he said, biting into a cleaned potato like it was an apple. "Don't let your parents tell you different."

While he ate he surveyed the sky, the dark slash of trees behind the garden. Mid-morning, and my excuses for him had run dry. A small anger ground like a heel in my stomach. While I sweated and dug, Uncle Norm leaned against his shovel and talked more movies with Pam. He'd also seen one about an earthquake that swallowed Los Angeles slowly into the ground. While you watched, quake vibrations boomed against the theatre's walls. They shook inside your chest. The audience clutched their seats and stared doubtfully at the ceiling. According to Uncle Norm, people who lived in glass houses perched on rocky bluffs were people waiting to die. They were alive, sure, but subconsciously they longed for the night the earth's force shook their beds through the walls and toppled them over the mountainside. "I think I might know that feeling," he said. He'd died—almost—so often his body felt stuck between life and death. He should be dead, but there he was, heart still clomping beneath his T-shirt. He pressed Pam's hand against his chest, letting her go only after she'd nodded, yes.

He paused for breath. Pam and I worked in silence. The sun

145

felt hotter, brighter, on the back of my neck. Finally, head bowed, Pam told him about her meningitis. "It was like being in a coma, only different, because I remember things," she said. She remembered dreaming about fuzzy men who smelled like ammonia trying to drag her under the bed. She also remembered our mother crying while this happened, although Pam couldn't tell if she'd been really crying or just in the dream. But these were all things that had happened to Pam, all things she couldn't talk about to anyone who hadn't almost died themselves. They wouldn't get it.

I kneeled, yanked a potato from its stubborn root. I didn't say a word. She wasn't talking to me, that was clear. Once I'd fallen from a tree branch and landed hard against the side of my face. This knocked me out. When I woke, Pam was leaned over me, shaking my shoulder, wet hair tucked behind her ears. Water beads dripped on my face and one ran inside my mouth, tasting tart with shampoo. I lay there unmoving, the world wrapped in gauze, and listened to Pam talk me out of the haze. But this seemed small next to what she and Uncle Norm had been through.

Eventually our mother hurried toward us wearing a dress and pink slippers. "Lunch is ready," she said. "And I think you need to help these children out some, Norm, if we're ever going to get the potatoes in."

He stared at his boots and said, "Yes, ma'am. It's just hard getting started sometimes, you know, my bones as old as they are."

"Norm," she said. "You've barely got three years on me."

Pam squinted like sun was in her eyes. "We're doing our best," she muttered. "And who's the one wearing slippers at high noon?"

Our mother's cheeks reddened. "I've worked damned hard

all morning in these slippers," she said. "There's soap waiting for you in the kitchen if you aren't careful." But all my mother's energy was gone by then.

Inside we ate bologna sandwiches and beans while our mother sat outside near the ditch, smoking and staring, as far as I could tell, at the telephone poles stuck in the ground. I saw her through the window, back turned away, wind blowing her dress in sad slow waves. I didn't feel hungry with her outside and that wind in her dress. I set down my sandwich and watched Uncle Norm scrape bread through the bean juice circling his plate. When he finished he reached into his pants pocket and held out a flat bottle the size of his hand. "Your father knows how to motivate a crew," Uncle Norm said.

Pam smiled, sort of, and I kept staring out at my mother. I thought I knew how she felt, alone outside, missing something she couldn't quite place. Uncle Norm poured a mouthful of whiskey into each of our glasses. "Drink up," he said. "Instant perk." And he tilted his glass into his mouth. Pam did the same and coughed. Uncle Norm smiled through his beard scruff. I waited until they were through, then swallowed mine down smoothly, without a grimace or any expression. No one noticed.

Our mother found out about the beer first.

Two days later, in fact, before noon, with the sky dumping so much rain, the garden turned into an ankle-sinking flat of mud. The rain meant no potato digging, so our mother kept Pam busy in the kitchen all morning, cleaning jars in steamy water. I lay on the living room sofa in front of a TV game show, idle, staring out at them. Our mother reached into the back of the refrigerator for two old jars of stewed tomatoes, now colored with blue fuzz. The jars were in her arms, she was backing away, when she paused. "One beer?" she said. At the sink, Pam's back stiffened. "I just put six in last night," she mumbled. "Your father had one, I had one." She looked at Pam. "Isn't that right?"

Pam shrugged, overcleaning the inside of a jar with a hard-bristled brush. "How should I know how much Dad drinks?" she said.

Our mother waited. "What's going on here?" she asked. "I'd care for the truth." Pam scrubbed and said nothing, so our mother swung her eyes suddenly, unexpectedly, toward me. How did I look, that caused an understanding to animate her face before she slammed down both jars, hard, on the kitchen table? A shiver shot up the jars into her arms. She charged to the basement and returned with all three truths clutched in her hands. "Excuse me," she mumbled to Pam through pressed lips, then drained the sink and emptied the slush from each bottle.

That night, she asked our father for a Discussion, so Pam and I went into the basement. The basement was Pam's choice, not mine. She sat on the sofa, hugging the pillow, her face tight. Uncle Norm sat in the corner chair, hands holding his knees. "Don't listen," he said. "It'll be over soon."

We couldn't not listen. "He's my only brother," our father said, voice rising. "What are you asking?" And our mother's voice, losing confidence: she couldn't take much more of Norm, sitting in the cellar with us children. She didn't trust him, telling us things, influencing us to steal from our parents, for God's sake. He had a bad effect, we were becoming undisciplined, couldn't our father see that? He had to listen.

After another moment, silent and long, we heard our father's footsteps move into the kitchen and our mother softly closing the bedroom door.

Later he came downstairs, holding the walls for support. I

shoved the pipe beneath my knee. Tired, newspaper drooping in his hand, our father waved Uncle Norm behind the stairs where, I suppose, he thought Pam and I wouldn't see. He forgot about the spaces between each step. So we watched him hand Uncle Norm his bottle, refilled. Uncle Norm nodded in a distant way, folded his fingers around it, held it for a long while between his hands. Our father suggested Uncle Norm leave the beer alone. "No one will notice the missing whiskey, do you see what I'm saying?" he said. Uncle Norm nodded again and they stood in silence, staring brother to brother in half-light.

Our father mumbled one word then. Soon?

Uncle Norm said, "Any time you want me to leave, you give me the word, Tom. You tell me straight."

Our father was powerless against such directness. I stared at my father and thought, *He's playing you.* Our father shook his head and said, "No. You can stay until you're ready to leave, of course."

After he'd gone I pulled out the pipe but didn't feel like chewing on anything of my father's. Uncle Norm walked back to us and thrust one leg onto the chair, then pulled it backwards toward him. "I'll be leaving soon, it seems," he said.

Pam squeezed the pillow still in her arms. "Maybe you could move into town," she mumbled. "Daddy would help you pay."

I didn't like the thought of Uncle Norm permanently nearby, a frequent holiday visitor, maybe, or a white-shirted member of our family every Sunday at church.

"I doubt that," Uncle Norm said. "But we might talk him into bringing you to the city for a visit sometime. You and the boy—" and he turned to me then, including me in one long look. "I'll take you to the Palace and we'll watch movies until morning. I'll save for that." I wanted to believe him, but who could be sure any more? He lowered his hand, just to squeeze

Pam's shoulder, but it ended up awkwardly placed against the back of her head. He patted her, then slipped his fingers through her hair. Pam continued looking into the pillow, not saying one thing or another.

Our mother didn't get out of bed the next morning. "I think I'll sleep in for awhile," she said when I checked on her. The bedroom shades were closed, so maybe she didn't notice the sun. "Help yourself to some cereal," she added, curled inside her sheets.

Uncle Norm lingered over breakfast since no adults were nearby. "It doesn't hurt anyone to sleep off the world for a day or two," he said. At the Y, he'd often sleep until afternoon or later. On his way to the community shower, he passed half-open doors and saw men still in bed, or sitting up but undressed, stomachs hanging in folds over their underwear, as though they were deciding whether they should bother standing. "Sometimes," he said, "it's all you've got to get you through a mood."

This is no Y, I thought but didn't say. Instead, I decided to dig potatoes. I sat on the floor, pushed on one boot, then the other. Beside Uncle Norm, Pam sullenly peeled a grapefruit. "It's too muddy," Uncle Norm said. "There'll be tons of mosquitoes, son." I looked back at him like nobody's son and sprayed bug disinfectant up and down my body until I smelled flammable.

Walking through the garden's mud was like walking in a dream, your legs moving heavy and slow. Mosquitoes swarmed around me but didn't land. I dug the potatoes and stacked them in one corner of the garden. After an hour my back cramped, but I didn't stop working. The pile of unearthed potatoes grew, my boots felt solid around my feet. Sweat clamped my shirt tight around my chest. I hoped my mother would open her bedroom shades and see me working, or see the potatoes waiting to be stored in the basement. I hoped Pam would come out and dig too. But none of these things happened. Outside it was me and the potatoes and the intermittent sun and the slow-drying mud.

I worked the entire morning and, at noon, went inside without being called. Uncle Norm stood over the kitchen stove, stirring soup. I ignored him, removed my boots and stocking-footed it to my mother's bedroom. Pam was there, holding a tall glass of lemonade. Two other glasses lined the dresser, one filled with milk, the other with orange juice. "She won't drink any of it," Pam said, biting her upper lip.

"Honey, I'm only resting," our mother mumbled. "Don't worry."

But she didn't sound normal, her voice barely a whisper. Both hands were pressed in a larger fist between her stomach and chest. "Is she sick?" Pam whispered, restless now. "If she is, we should call a doctor. Or Daddy."

I pictured our father driving home, leaping from the car, running long-legged to the bedroom, and our mother sitting up, saying, "I'm fine, Tom," and choosing one of Pam's three drinks. I pictured the accusing look on her face. "She said she wasn't sick," I said.

Pam continued watching the bed, dissatisfied. Finally our mother turned over, smiled loosely at the two of us. "If I drink something, will you not worry, dear?" she asked.

"Drink the juice," Pam said, shoving that glass into our mother's hand. "It's the best for you."

"Because really I'm fine. I'm only trying to relax and think about things. Adults do that sometimes."

The first thing our mother saw when sitting up was Uncle Norm, now in the doorway. He held a plate with a white ceramic bowl in the center. The spoon inside the bowl radiated the soup's heat, I thought, that's why it shined so. "Don't worry,

151

Irene," he said. "I'm bringing this to you."

He walked forward, balancing the bowl. Steam curled behind him, then disappeared. Our mother's smile shrunk by half and stiffened. "What's this?" she asked.

"Soup," he said. "Chicken and dumplings. There's also some for the children, soon as they want some lunch." He stood over the bed, the smell of basement dampness inside his clothes, the soup unsteady in his hands. Our mother kicked free of the bed sheets, legs blue with tiny arcing veins.

"I don't care for any soup," she said.

"She's drinking juice," Pam said. And our mother did, an obligation, but she didn't move her eyes once from Uncle Norm. I had looked at dentists with drills spinning in their hands that same way. When she was through she handed the clotted glass back to Pam. "Now that I've had my juice like a good mother, I'd appreciate being left alone for awhile, Norm," she said. "If you wouldn't mind."

Instead of exiting discreetly, Uncle Norm sat on the bed, face stiffening around his eyes and mouth. Dumplings bobbed on the surface of the soup now balanced on his lap. "I think you should have some, Irene," he said. "I made this for you."

Our mother smiled wildly, as if she thought his persistence was a strange joke, then he said, "I'm serious," and her smile faded. She shook her head, lay back down. "Please go," she said. "I'm tired."

Now Uncle Norm leaned over her, soup cradled at his chest. "I'm tired, too," he said. "Of this way you're acting toward me. I'm trying to *feed* you, is all."

The room closed in around us. I wanted to push him away, I was dizzy with this urge, and at that same moment, nearly in slow motion, Pam lifted her hands and did push him, once, solidly against the shoulders. He backed off, soup swelling over the sides and dribbling on the edge of the bed. "Don't!" she whispered. "She said she didn't want any."

After that things changed, although Uncle Norm's immediate response was to level Pam in a glance, set the steaming bowl beside the glasses and return to the cellar. He stayed there all afternoon, though, and in the evening, when our father called him for the supper our mother had climbed from bed to scrape together, he still wouldn't come. Later, our father went down to him. Sighing, our mother sink-stacked the dishes, then wandered back toward the bedroom. "Tomorrow's wash," she said over her shoulder without seeing us. "Get your clothes ready."

Pam and I sat in front of the TV, waiting for something. The sun was setting, filling the room with red light. When our father came upstairs and found our mother in bed, he stared around the empty kitchen like there was something special he was searching for. He went outside until the sun had dropped fully behind the trees, then came back in, scratching fresh mosquito bites, and went to bed too. Pam and I looked at each other. It was barely nine.

Eventually Pam went downstairs for Uncle Norm's dirty laundry. I started going with her but stopped halfway, confused. I didn't want to talk to him. I had nothing to say. So I watched from the steps as Pam lifted his discarded clothes off the floor, chairs, table tops. "Mom's washing tomorrow," she said. "We'll do yours too." Uncle Norm lay on the sofa, arms crossed. He might have nodded, but I couldn't be sure. Pam mumbled a few words I couldn't hear. He remained still, though, eyes set on the pipes overhead. He refused to look at her or me, wavering on the steps.

When she came back up, her arms were heaped with limp jeans, shirts, rolled socks that smelled sour. "Is he okay?" I asked.

It took her awhile to shake her head. "He's not talking," she said. "I even asked him about a movie. I don't care though. He can be any weird way he wants."

And she went upstairs with Uncle Norm's clothes pressed against her chest.

Three other things happened that night.

I grew bored with TV, went upstairs to Pam's room and caught her tilting Uncle Norm's whiskey flask into her mouth. "Major find," she said. "Left jacket pocket." She was wearing a bathrobe and brushing her hair between sips, Uncle Norm's clothes piled on her bed.

"You're not drinking that stuff?" I asked.

A meanness lighted her eyes. "You're getting slower every day. You do it like this." She poured whiskey into the bottle cap and swallowed it hard, like a medicine.

"I know how to drink," I said. So she held out the bottle, as in, show me. I didn't want to disappoint her, but still. I shuffled my feet.

"Then go away," she said, "because I intend to read and get very drunk."

I didn't go, though, not right away. Pam didn't force me. She brushed her hair until it crackled, then giggled. "I think I'm drunk," she said. "I think I'm very drunk. I feel like I should be dancing or something." But she didn't, just stood holding the brush, an ivory white weight in her hand. "Do you think he meant it?" she asked. "About taking us to the movies? I'd love to see the Palace."

"I don't think I'd count on him," I said.

154

That wasn't the answer she wanted, because her eyes turned hard again. "Didn't I want to be alone to read and get very drunk?" she said. Eyeing the movie magazines on her shelf, she dropped to her knees suddenly and yanked out the two magazines holding up her bed. I left her there, magazines in hand, staring me down the stairs and away from her, bed tilted to one side.

Later, feeling down and lonely, I tiptoed to the living room chute with my own laundry and heard Uncle Norm's voice, rising up: "Pam! Pamela!" I froze. His was a rich dreamy whisper, flung far back in his throat. Had he noticed the missing bottle? Did he want a beer? Was he sorry for not talking to Pam? I backed away with my arms still laundry-heavy. I left him down there to call.

And I had trouble sleeping that night. Outside crickets shrilled beneath my window. At least one had found its way into my room. I heard it chirping somewhere near the closet, possibly in my dirty clothes. I was afraid I'd fall asleep, wake to it crawling up my bare arm, leg, a whisper of movement across my skin. When finally I did sleep, I dreamed of me and Pam and Uncle Norm under the Palace's hot lights. Uncle Norm paid our way and seated me inside, his bony fingers urging me down. Then he dragged Pam to the projection booth by her hair, leaving me alone in the dark surrounded by strangers who smelled like animals. When I woke I strained my ears— because wasn't that him, really, in the kitchen, moving, while the rest of us lay sluggish and low-spirited in our beds? I listened, hard, but heard only crickets and the sound of pipes. The night stretched on, jerking me in and out of dreams. Finally, in early morning, I pitched into a sleep that left even dreaming behind.

First I heard shuffles, the whisper of my mother's voice. I couldn't hear her words. A door closed. Someone coughed, then I heard someone throwing up. I knew something was happening, I should wake up now, but I couldn't pull myself fully out of sleep. It pressed down inside me, nailing me to the bed. Thickheaded, I listened. More coughing. Pam was sick. I had a dream image of her on her knees, bright strands of hair stabbing at her mouth. I remembered last night then, Uncle Norm's bottle and her drinking. I sat up.

I waited a minute for my head to clear. "Can I come in, Pam?" my mother was saying as I shook my legs into a pair of jeans and barefooted into the hall. "To check on you?"

The bathwater was running, I heard that. And Pam's feet shuffling across the bathroom tiles. She opened the door and I saw her briefly, hair in her face, eyes gray and sluggish. I smelled her too, a light sourness through the door. "I'm taking a bath, Ma," she said. "I'll be fine after a bath."

She closed the door before we could answer. My mother and I stood for a moment, then she smiled faintly at me. In the kitchen she shovelled coffee grounds into the percolator. If my head had been lighter, clearer, I would have appreciated that she was out of bed and moving around. "Maybe we'll get the potatoes in today, if Pam's okay," I mumbled.

She lit a cigarette, pushed two pieces of bread into the toaster. It was mid-morning but felt earlier, just before dawn, when the air is still empty of human sound. "Pam shouldn't be out in the garden today," she said. The bread popped up, lightly toasted, and she overbuttered each slice, cigarette seesawing between her fingers. "Your sister gets sick easily," she added.

I sat on my chair. I realized then I was shirtless. I stared at my chest, arms, like it was not my bare skin. *At some point my head will shake clear of this,* I thought. When that happened, I would put on my shirt.

My mother stared out the kitchen window toward the road. She peeled the crust off her toast, stuffed it torn and ragged into her mouth. "Pam, don't use all the water please!" she called.

The bathwater was still running, a soothing sound. I thought of small waterfalls dropping into a larger stream. My mother and I sat for a couple of dizzying minutes, just listening and watching the sun push farther into the room. My mother shook her head suddenly, wiped crumbs from her hands and walked to the bathroom door. "Pamela, I mean it," she said, knocking. "There's a water shortage."

Pam didn't answer. The water answered with its steady falling.

Our mother pushed the door open and walked in. And even her first scream didn't kick me back to full reality. I couldn't respond because it didn't seem real. But her second scream jolted through the full length of me, and I was on my feet, running into the bathroom.

I saw my mother pulling Pam by the hair from the tub. The bath was so full, water spilled over the edges. I turned off the nozzles just as my mother's final pull dropped Pam to the floor, her shoulders wetly smacking against the tiles. Dimly I saw her breasts, white and wet, and the hair between her legs. Then our mother rolled Pam onto her stomach and slapped between her shoulders. Twice, hard. "Pam!" she said. "Pam, wake up!"

I kneeled beside them, heart pounding. My mother rolled Pam face up again. She was still, her skin and lips tinged blue. "My God," our mother said, face breaking, hands rising to her mouth. "Pam, please."

From somewhere I thought to lower my mouth over Pam's and breathe in, out, the way I'd seen done in the movies. It wasn't so hard, because I couldn't feel myself moving or breathing her full of air. I couldn't think of the taste inside her mouth—whiskey, the sour of vomit. I only breathed. Finally bath water passed from Pam's mouth into mine. I spit it out, then turned her head sideways so the water would trickle onto the tiles.

"She's breathing," our mother said. "She breathed, I saw her." Still Pam didn't open her eyes. Our mother was crying by then, hugging her arms and leaning forward. I shook Pam's shoulder. This time we could touch her. And what I said was, "Pam, come on. Can you get up?"

First she blinked, then, almost reluctantly, opened her eyes. They rolled back into her whites, focused and stared up at me. "Christ," she whispered, arms covering her nakedness. Then she dragged herself to the stool to cough up more bath water.

Trembling, our mother picked up Pam's bathrobe and held it out to cover her. Our mother must have felt its heaviness, because she paused, then reached inside the pocket and removed Uncle Norm's flask. The bottle looked liquidy, a small and fragile thing in her hand. She stared at it until she'd made the connection, then tossed the flask into the bathtub. She plunged her arm elbow-deep into the water and pulled the plug, not bothering to lift her sleeve first. She hurried into the living room and pushed the heavy china cabinet against the basement door. I felt its clawed feet shaking the floor. Finally she phoned our father. "Come take this brother of yours away now or I'm leaving with the children," she said. "He's almost drowned our daughter."

Uncle Norm wasn't surprised when our father returned from work and told him he had to leave, today, so pack up. But he was confused when, outside by the car, he asked to say goodbye to Pam

158

and our father refused. "I would like to see Pam and have a smoke before I go, Tom," was how he asked.

Our father lit a cigarette and handed it to him.

So Uncle Norm leaned toward me. "Tell your sister if you ever get this father of yours to take you into the city, I'll be near the Palace," he said. "Will you do that?" He winked, maybe trying to rib the sternness from my father's face. But this time, my father was unyielding. He opened the car door for Uncle Norm and they drove off, Uncle Norm's blank pale face staring out the window at me. I knew that was the last I'd see of him, so I watched the car disappear around the curve in the road.

Late that afternoon, when Pam woke, I told her Uncle Norm had gone. She nodded, unsurprised, and stared out the window for a long while. Then she started talking about the bathtub. She remembered water lapping at her legs, swelling over her belly. Her head had felt so heavy! She'd closed her eyes and imagined herself on a beach, full of shells and whispers and secret things. The surf broke, grew stronger, loosened the sand around her. It pulled her out. Then she was simply part of water, around and inside her. She yielded, floated on a wave toward darkness. In the end, what she heard was someone calling her back to shore and the air.

I nodded but said nothing. We both stared out at the garden, the potato stack, the twisted tree branches tapping against the windows. Downstairs our parents were talking, so low we couldn't hear their words. That was a new sound.

"Did he ask about me?" Pam said. I paused, deciding between several possible answers. "He said goodbye," I told her.

That night our father decided we should go to a movie. "Doesn't hurt to treat every now and then, does it?" he asked when we stared at him, stunned. In the car he played the radio

159

loud, humming under his breath. At the theatre window he said, "Four, please," and fingered the bills in his wallet, like this was something he'd always done.

And we sat there in the dark together, my family and I. My father had the aisle seat, a smile plastered across his face over this extravagant gift he'd given his family. My mother sat next to him, the perfect moviegoer—she laughed and cried in the right places, she ate from the small bucket of popcorn teetering in her lap. She didn't pull away when our father rested his buttery hand on her knee. Pam came next, breath held, eyes fixed on the screen like she expected it to evaporate in front of her.

I sat on the inside, watching my family as well as the movie. I stared also at the shadows of others in the theatre, strangers really, until we were all gathered in this place for a movie, and then they were like people I knew. But even while the movie played, I knew inside myself this would soon end. The doors would open, we would be ushered back into the night and the dazed unlucky lives we all endured separately. I thought about this for only a moment, then yielded to the movie like everyone else. I watched those people on the screen. I listened to their voices, stronger and clearer than ours—voices that for one night, anyway, called my family back to life.

Waiting for the End

The summer she was waiting for her boyfriend to return home, Meridel began spending time with Boyd Murphy. Boyd was nineteen, weedy and contemplative and even good-looking— and dying. He wasn't dying anytime soon, necessarily, but he might also die tomorrow. At least that was the word around. He lived with his mother, a lean, severe-looking woman with small cramped teeth and a pointed chin, whose husband, Boyd's father, had also died of leukemia, many years ago. Actually, the leukemia had begun with Boyd's great grandfather in an earlier century, and had been passed down, with increasing strength, from great grandfather to grandfather to father to, finally, Boyd himself. Living around so much death, *persistent* death, had damaged Mrs. Murphy somewhat, had fueled her moods and rancor, or so Meridel imagined. Being the lone survivor was wearing on her.

Meridel was twenty eight and lived alone in a small rental next door. Weeds were all that separated her house from theirs, until the day in late June when she returned from work, in a light harmless rain, and saw Boyd on his knees, digging up these weeds with a rusty trowel.

Normally Meridel did not linger with Boyd—his condition disquieted her, and who knew where the mother might be?—but that day she needed to talk to someone, *anyone,* and Boyd was there. Work had been intolerable, for one thing. First she'd spilled coffee down the front of her dress, leaving a visible brown stain. One couple felt she hadn't serviced them hospitably enough and ratted on her to the cashier. By afternoon she had mistotaled four bills, and was four times offered the correct sum by her offended customers. Finally the manager lost patience and commanded her back into the kitchen, where he scolded her as if she were a trainee, as if she hadn't been working there for six full years. Six years! Meridel gazed at the hissing grills, the dingy glasses and dishes awaiting their dunks in water too murky to see through, and she thought, *This is my whole life.* Now that her so-called boyfriend, Kyle, wasn't around, what did she do with her time besides work? She could answer that. She waited to hear from him. Later, while she was still thinking these things, a customer waved her over and held up his fork. "There's yolk here!" he said. "Look between the spaces and tell me what you see." She didn't look, of course, just snatched the fork from his hand, walked it back to the kitchen and flung it at the boy spraying plates with a long snakey nozzle.

Besides, she wasn't sure she could bear another night, alone in her house, waiting for the phone to ring. So she watched Boyd, his movements graceful and drawn-out, even focused, as if nothing existed but he and the weeds. "I hope those aren't my weeds you're being forced to dig up," she said.

Boyd looked up, shielding his eyes with one hand, though there was no sun, the sky was completely clouded over and gray.

"No," he said. "These weeds belong to no one, they're just here."

She liked the sound of those words—*these weeds belong to no one, they're just here*—and repeated them in her mind. They were the most interesting words she'd heard all day, at any rate. She didn't answer him, though, for she didn't consider herself gifted with words. Apparently nothing she'd said to Kyle before he left, or wrote in her long and, what she considered, impassioned letters, had made much of an impression.

"Should you be out in the rain, Boyd?" she asked, then cringed. Saying his name in this way—Boyd?—definitely smacked of solicitousness. But how did one talk to the terminally ill with any kind of ease? "It's just that a lot of people have been coming down with the flu. Two girls at work are out with it."

White grass-smeared gardening gloves encased what she imagined were his meek and slender hands. He lifted a small pile of weeds and dumped these into a larger pile beside him. "Flu is the least of my worries," he said. His laughter was genuine, but swift, economical, and in a moment he was silent again. Yet Meridel was startled, even embarrassed by the sound.

"Besides, when the ground's wet, weeds pull up easier," Boyd continued. "Not that weeds take much effort anyway. They don't have a deep root system. That's why they flourish."

Meridel nodded, waited, then realized their conversation was finished.

Still, something unspoken had started between them, though Meridel did not realize this until later that same evening, when Boyd brought over a small pile of her clothes, neatly folded. "I forgot to give you these this afternoon," he said. "My mind was on other things."

Meridel stared, confused. In his hands the clothes didn't look like hers. They appeared fresh, well-cared for, a stranger's prettier things.

"You left them hanging out," he said. "When the rain started up and you weren't here, I decided to bring them in for you. They were flapping so."

"That was thoughtful," she mumbled. He passed her the clothes, but stood in the kitchen for longer than the transaction required. "Now I'm off," he said, nodding and backing away with his hands shoved firmly in his pockets.

Later, she wished she'd offered him something—soda, maybe, or a handful of trail mix, which at the time had been in a bowl at the center of the table. The mix and a glass of juice was meant to be her supper, but she'd been thinking too much about Kyle; then, realizing this, she had struggled to think of other things. As usual her mind locked in the conflict and she forgot both eating and amenity. By ten o'clock she was tired and bored and restless with a longing that had been with her for weeks, so she dismissed Kyle from her thoughts and prepared for bed. As soon as the lights were out, though, her mind retreated, without mercy, back to Kyle.

He had been gone for six weeks now, and she hadn't heard from him for five. She had received a postcard the first week. *I'm in Kansas now,* he wrote. *Passing through for Tulsa. This statue reminded me of you. Take care, bun* and his name, Kyle. The statue was a soldier with a stone cape chiseled high over one shoulder, who gazed intrepidly into a landscape the card did not picture. Behind the statue was a munitions plant. She couldn't imagine how this statue reminded Kyle of her. Nothing in their relationship—nothing—made her think of this or any statue. She had puzzled about this for awhile, even committed herself to asking him about it when he called, except that he never had.

"I need to take a little road trip, bunny," he'd said a couple weeks before his departure. Possibly she should have suspected something then, because he never called her bunny. "Drive around the country for awhile. Step on some new land before I'll ever decide about us."

Decide about them? She had never asked him to decide about them, though it was true, she often daydreamed about a more permanent life with him. They would probably live in this same town but a different house than hers, and they would work separately but return home, wearied, to each other every night. A typical evening would include a nap, a jointly-cooked supper and, finally, television. She pictured endless summer and winter nights like this, on the sofa holding each other, watching TV characters facing complication upon complication, only to solve them all within sixty minutes. During the less interesting shows she might doze off to a silent and lonely place inside herself, then wake with a start and he would be right there, heart knocking against his chest where her ear was pressed. Hers were simple, even mundane longings, she realized this, but she couldn't help wanting them.

"You don't understand," he'd said. "I'm dreaming about hills and long sloping roads and the road turns to sand, I can't pedal my bike through it, then I'm on foot and the sand turns to rock and I'm crawling, then its a little mountain and I'm climbing it, trying to reach the top, but it's getting steeper, till pretty soon I'm climbing straight up, then the mountain is so steep it's curving behind me, so I can't see ahead of where I'm crawling. Do you see what I mean? All the while someone's gaining on me."

"Who's that chasing you?" she asked.

He shrugged. "I don't think it's any one someone," he said. "It's a shadow. A form. You know how dreams are."

167

He'd talked in this manner for most of the night, and by morning he'd quit his job and was humming, though this melody didn't include her. When he looked at her or kissed her cheek with careless vigor, he could have been kissing anyone—a sister or visiting cousin. The suddenness of his change numbed her. By the time she realized she would have been within her rights to ask him to stay, or at least ask to join him, he had gone.

Now Meridel dozed briefly, then woke feeling stuck, rootless. There was no reason for her to be in this town! she thought hotly. None. She snapped on the lamp, frightened. The room was shadowy, deep, and everything looked impersonal. The dresses hanging from her open closet, her shoes neatly lined below them—all these things she had bought herself. None had been given to her out of love or affection. Boyd returning her things this evening, that was the closest she had come. She wandered to the bathroom. In the mirror her face shown pale and thin and, yes, desperate. She thought her name at the face in the mirror: Meridel. If things weren't trying enough, there was her name: it belonged to an old woman, an organizer of church retreats, certainly not to a woman with yearnings and a life still ahead of her.

She sat up for awhile, thinking these things. The bed was empty and looked forlorn. The sheets still smelled of Kyle, despite repeated washings. She couldn't return to the bed yet. Waking in it, alone, aroused a panic she could never control. So she sat on a chair and gazed through the window facing the Murphy's house. A single light spilled from a corner window she imagined was not a bedroom, but was, instead, the living room, where Boyd was reading quietly into the night, filling up the hours, death giving him the impetus to live fully and with discipline. Why should such a thought soothe her—a dying

168

young man reading beside a lamp in an otherwise dark house? She was becoming increasingly enigmatic, even to herself. *Imagine what he dreams,* she thought.

She decided to sit until the light went off and he'd gone to bed. But she waited and waited, and when the light still shined, she gave up this idea, too, and returned to bed on her own volition.

And though there was no definite transition into it, they soon began spending their free time together.

The summer was wet and stormy. Several nights a week it would rain, sometimes ruthlessly, lashing the trees and a field of young corn visible from Meridel's porch. Other times, the rain was placid and benign, with only the best intentions.

Usually Boyd would visit Meridel. In fact, she had been to his place only once, and Mrs. Murphy had ruined the atmosphere between them. The Murphy's did not have a porch so she and Boyd had been sitting in the living room, trying to make themselves heard above the pots and pans Mrs. Murphy was banging in and out of the kitchen cupboards. What was she doing? Meridel wondered. Removing them all for a communal washing? Stacking them by size? "I'm not sure I've ever felt really alive," Boyd had said. "Even as a boy, I knew I was marked." The kitchen noises stopped abruptly and then Mrs. Murphy was leaning over them with a Teflon skillet in her hand. "Boyd, for Christ's sake," she whispered. "What are you saying? You barely know Meridel. What a thing to say to her when you've just become acquainted." Her face had been apologetic, flushed. Blue splotches colored her cheeks and temples and neck.

So they preferred sitting on Meridel's porch and watching the storms push in. Meridel opened all her windows and doors, wanting the wild wet smell of the passing storms inside her house. Also, she would hear the phone if it rang.

One night lightning pierced the sky in all directions, and for two seconds everything shone white and defined. Telephone poles, wires, fields, the wind-bowed trees—all stood momentarily stark against an alien landscape.

"Lightning doesn't look the way it used to, that's for sure," Boyd said. He sat on the floor, leaning against the ripped screen door. He wore jeans and a frayed white shirt. "Lightning used to look more *distant*. I remember it striking higher in the sky, somehow. Lately, it seems to strike very close to the ground."

"Maybe the land is flatter here," she said, sipping from the glass of Tab. "Or something. Maybe it's just more noticeable."

Boyd shrugged. "It's true, I haven't always lived here."

Actually, he'd lived the first few years of his life in Ohio. He had memories of Ohio, but only one stuck out with any clarity.

"I remember a thunderstorm," Boyd said. "Across from our house was a field, and in this field was a big tree. Just one tree. Ma always told me I had to stay away from it during a storm, because that tree was a fire hazard. During a storm, she said, that was the most likely place for lightning to strike. Of anywhere around. So one afternoon, when she was napping, a storm rolled in and I just ran out, in all that rain, to stand beneath the tree. I couldn't resist the danger. You know how kids are."

He paused. She was expected to add to the conversation. "I was a kid once myself," she tried, staring down at her glass. Her fingers had smudged it beyond what she could account for. Her hands were not unclean.

"Anyway, I stood there, and then I stood there and stood there, and *nothing*. Lightning didn't hit the tree or anything around. It didn't come close. I was pretty pissed. Lightning

170

didn't seem all that dangerous to me. Sure it looked scary, but it was too far off for anyone to get bent out of shape about. Even standing in the most dangerous place seemed like no big deal." Boyd scratched his arm. "My Dad was still alive then, too," he added.

More lightning streaked the sky, only this time it did not split apart—it was yellow and singular, gentle really, soft as the snap of a camera. "Do you remember him pretty well?" she asked.

"I remember him alright. The memory's there but gets cloudier every year." Boyd removed a pack of cigarettes, lit one, and inhaled. "I take that right back. Over the past months, it's starting to get sharper again, do you know what I mean?"

She wasn't sure, so she said, "Should you be smoking?"

"What difference does it make? What does smoking have to do with leukemia, anyway?" He asked this seriously, his face drawn into tight quizzical lines. "You worry too much about the wrong things, Meridel."

"I do not!" she protested. Still, she liked the way her name sounded coming from his mouth, and the way his mouth looked, saying it.

"I'm dying early, I know it, so what good is worrying about my body now? My body's betrayed me. I owe it nothing." Boyd's cigarette gleamed, a tiny dour eye observing her in the dark. It began to rain, but not viciously. Meridel placed her bare feet across the porch railing, trying to figure why it did matter to her, knowing it did not matter to him. Maybe it was because she was years older than he was. Then again, this didn't seem a good explanation at all. "So what ever happened to him?" Boyd asked.

Meridel stiffened. "Who?"

"Don't be elusive. Him. I don't see him around anymore."

171

"Kyle's taken a trip," she said. "He's gone off to see a few things, then he's coming back and we're going to be married."

Instantly she was alarmed, hearing this swift lie push so naturally from her mouth. And she had lied to a dying person, which seemed more wrong—desperate—than lying to just anyone.

"As soon as he comes back," she added, playing it through, though she was disappointed with herself, her haste and lack of imagination.

There was a silence between them.

"There's nothing wrong with plans," Boyd said.

And another night he said, in part, ". . . I have no plans, you see. I live each day without expectation but with complete acceptance."

Meridel nodded, unable to place what had prompted this remark. They had not been talking about anything so serious. They'd been sharing swimming stories. Boyd had not been allowed to swim as a child. He'd always wanted to know that feeling: his body, buoyant, in deep water. Meridel told him about a time she was young, maybe thirteen, and had been forced to swim with a group of children. She'd stood on the beach, already self-conscious of herself in a bathing suit, and terrified of going into water above her chest, while the other kids dove and stroked and butterflied and taunted her. It would not have been so much if a boy she rather liked—reckless tow-haired Ted—hadn't been there, too, immersed to his neck, grinning at her with a sunny contempt when she plugged her nose and dipped her face into the water, trying to please them, please *him*, and coming up gasping, dripping, clutching herself while they laughed. She could never look Ted in the face after this, knowing how he'd seen her in comparison to how she'd wanted to be seen.

It was much later, after Boyd had returned home and Meridel was lying in her empty bed, that she realized they'd actually been talking about desire.

In church one Sunday, during the reading of the Psalms, Meridel saw Mrs. Murphy sneak in late—panting, face flushed— without Boyd. Startled, Meridel lost the refrain and couldn't continue. She kept glancing back, somewhat conspicuously, at Mrs. Murphy. She looked disheveled, even peaked; she dabbed at her face with a clot of blue tissue but stared with a fixed, singular commitment at the pulpit.

The whole side of her pew was empty, missing Boyd.

During coffee hour, Mrs. Murphy sat alone, eating a muffin. The truth was, most people avoided her, not just Meridel. Her angry face, her moods, and then her son dying in front of her— this did not inspire Sunday palaver. Today, though, Meridel was driven. "Where's Boyd?" she asked.

Mrs. Murphy took an exact bite from her muffin.

"I hope he's okay."

"He's fine. Believe me. Apparently he's outgrown worship, is all."

Meridel said "oh" and stared down at the table. J.M. had been carved deeply into one corner. It was a shame, how much effort must have gone into this, how much care and exertion, only to have the results emerge so misshaped.

"Perhaps you've had something to do with this?" Mrs. Murphy asked. "That would be one explanation."

"Of course not. I don't have that kind of influence over him."

"Really? Well, there's a surprise." The remainder of the

173

muffin crumbled in Mrs. Murphy's fingers. She dropped the crumbs into her napkin, rubbed her fingers together, folded the napkin into a knot, then lifted her head very high, as if trying to pinpoint an unexpected sound. "This is not the time he should be rejecting anything, of course, much less God. For Heaven's sake."

Until now Meridel had never noticed how soft Mrs. Murphy's neck looked. When she lifted her chin, tiny veins stretched blue and weary beneath her skin. Meridel found herself wishing Mrs. Murphy would swallow, just once more.

"Maybe it's a phase," Mrs. Murphy said. "That's possible. A phase in his journey toward acceptance. Don't you think that could be it?"

Fortunately, before Meridel was required to respond, Mrs. Murphy stood and, with the poise of a woman who had finished her business, walked from the church.

As it turned out, Boyd had not rejected God or any such thing. "I've given up on church, is all," he said. "It doesn't yield for me. Words aren't enough anymore."

Again they were sitting on the porch, and again Boyd was smoking and she was drinking Tab, only now there was no storm, the night was still except for the hum of bugs—the crickets and grasshoppers and mosquitoes.

"I don't want to hear promises," Boyd continued. "I'm past that."

The porch floor was littered with his cigarette butts. Dimly Meridel realized he hadn't been careful about picking up after himself over the past few days, and she had not noticed. Her mind had been elsewhere, shifting from thought to thought, but apparently not to the porch floor.

"It's hard to explain," Boyd continued. "I want things to be

174

more *personal*. I want to experience everything in a new way. I'm tired of the old ways. The old ways have buried me."

"Of course." Meridel was untroubled by his answers, even reassured, though she couldn't help feeling a small stubborn loyalty to the church. And she couldn't add to his random philosophies. This was another thing missing in her life, she thought bleakly—not just Kyle, but philosophies. All she had were harsh and melancholy longings, grinding inside her, scraping her heart raw.

"I would like Ma to understand this, but I think she's pretty set in the ways of this life." Boyd pressed out another cigarette between the floor boards. "She's always believed in the idea of intercession."

Intercession? To Meridel the word itself sounded suspicious.

"I was afraid when your mother walked in alone," she said, pressing the glass against her dry hands.

Boyd spread his hand flat across the unvarnished boards.

Meridel gazed through a space between these boards. She saw beneath her feet an object, dully glistening in the dirt, but she could not make the object out. "I was afraid something had happened to you," she murmured. "I was afraid it was time."

He nodded, his hand still in place over the boards, as if it were someone's skin he was touching.

"I wouldn't go before letting you know," he said. "Don't you know that? Give me a little control over this scenario, anyway."

Mrs. Murphy pulled up in front of the house just then. She parked but sat in the car for awhile, head bowed, hands still clutching the wheel. Then she stared over her shoulder at them, without acknowledgement. When she stepped from the car, finally, her eyes still upon them, she held a grocery bag in her arms. Her scarf was blue, though appeared silver in the light from the street lamp. Meridel wondered how she and Boyd

175

looked from the street—were they a comforting sight or a sad one? Heat lightning flashed behind Mrs. Murphy.

"You two," she said, shaking her head.

On nights when Boyd did not come over, or when he was in the hospital for overnight monitoring or simply had other obligations, which was not all that often but sometimes, Meridel sat on the porch alone, or at the kitchen table with the newspaper spread out, unread, before her. She was never sure what she was reading for and this drove her a little crazy. It was like her nights before she'd begun hanging with Boyd—long, shapeless, futile. She knew it was senseless to be this way, but she had no way of controlling herself, it seemed. She played the radio a lot—sixties ballads and jazz, mostly. A few times she went out and snipped at her overgrown bushes, but usually went inside after a few minutes, feeling dowdy, her arms itching. Once she started walking toward downtown, then became frightened that she was away and wouldn't know if something happened. She hurried back, drew a bath and cried briefly while the yellow water rose around her.

Another night the phone rang. Meridel was so startled, she didn't answer it. What if it was Kyle? What if it wasn't? She sat in the kitchen long after the frustrated phone stopped ringing, caught in this indefinite state—surely, she thought, this couldn't go on. Through her window she heard Mrs. Murphy banging her pots and pans. Meridel no longer cared about the reasons for this cacophony. The angry clanging sounds made her feel oddly justified. She closed her eyes and listened.

When Meridel woke early one Friday to an ambulance light chopping the air red in front of the Murphy's, her breath stalled and she instantly felt Boyd's absence, the lack of him nearby.

176

Struggling into her bathrobe, she rushed through the sluggish house, thinking herself foolish for trusting he had enough control to warn her about this.

She stumbled barefoot onto the lawn and watched two grave ambulance men carrying Mrs. Murphy from the house on a stretcher. Her hair was unwashed and unbrushed. A small plastic breathing cup, attached to a tube on wheels, covered her face. *She looks tired and peaceful,* Meridel thought wildly.

Boyd followed, buttoning his shirt, hair askew. "Her heart," he whispered to Meridel, looking as though he didn't recognize her. Dry brown sleep crusted his eyelids. Meridel lifted her fingers instinctively to his face, then stopped and stared at her outstretched hands. *No!* she thought at them.

"She woke for her shower and fell seconds after she'd closed the bathroom door. I heard the water glass breaking. That's how I knew she needed me."

Boyd rode to the hospital in the ambulance, kneeled beside his mother, and holding her, and talking her through this scene he knew so well. That was how Meridel imagined Boyd, anyway, as she hurried through her morning shower, ate a wilted piece of toast, phoned in sick from work, and drove toward the hospital, feeling both dread and an odd release. Freedom, almost. She hadn't driven in this direction at sunrise for some time. The town looked different than she remembered. The sky was flushed with a young and hopeful sun that lighted the roofs, the peeled buildings, turning them shiny and clean. Two teenaged girls passed her car, laughing, gesturing, their arms jangling with bracelets, their hair twisted in daring braids that jostled down the middle of their backs. Watching them, Meridel felt almost happy.

She tried carrying the memory of the girls and the braids into the hospital with her, but hospitals were so overwhelming!

177

The hard clinical light sterilized everything in sight. Soon she felt unclean, walking through the immaculate halls. She sat beside Boyd on a tiny armless sofa near his mother's room. "I see now I've been misguided," he whispered, flipping through a magazine he wasn't reading. "I've been approaching death on trust, like there's a reason for it beyond my understanding. Now I see it's really a phantom. A robber. There's no real pattern of selectivity. It comes, takes, and then it goes. This isn't news to most people. I'm afraid I've been somewhat arrogant."

"Don't be so hard on yourself," she said. But these words, too, sounded stilted, and not all that insightful. They were the words any stranger might just as easily have chosen. She stood and poured a Dixie cup of water for Boyd. The water was cloudy, even chalky, but he drank without complaint. Later, though, when she would get him another cup, she would walk to the dispenser at the end of the hall, where the water was always cool and clear.

Together, they waited for an hour, then another. Meridel felt disconnected from things. She wasn't sure if this was because she'd been startled awake this morning, or if it was the circumstances—being inside this hospital instead of at the restaurant, going through the drudgery to which her body was accustomed. The sun poured through a window onto her lap, and suddenly it had slipped behind a church steeple across the street and the room was cooler. She looked out the window, feeling cheated. "You don't have to stay," Boyd said. "You must have better things to do than wait around here with me."

"Oh no," she said. "Not really." As it was, she felt comfortable waiting with him. Waiting was what she knew best. And she couldn't imagine not being here with him. Who else was there?

178

When she grew tired, she moved to another chair where there was still sun, leaned her head back, and closed her eyes. She dreamed lightly, but all her dreams were of birds, flying low over cornfields or bursting from the thunderclouds, flying in dark uneven lines in every direction. She dreamed of the baby sparrow she had found as a girl and housed in a box, feeding it and loving it. Two days later, it died. "It needed its mother, honey," her mother had said. "You couldn't give it the kind of love it needed."

Meridel woke feeling some great loss had already occurred, years before Kyle, that had been buried inside her since she was a child and, possibly, even before then. Blinking from the sun, she watched three doctors walking in harmony down the long hallway. They gathered around Boyd. The sun gleamed off their white lab coats. It hurt her to look in their direction. Boyd stood with dignity to greet them. As if from a distance, she heard them tell Boyd his mother was dead.

Now it was late August and the storms were zeroing in for a furious final lashing. Needle-sharp rain pummelled the ground with a score to settle. It pounded onto roofs and rivered through gutters. Thunder crackled and, twice, blackened out electricity across town. Houses stood dark and small and emptied. All light was in the sky.

In this weather, Mrs. Murphy was buried. Ten people attended the funeral, including Meridel and Boyd but not including the reverend. Boyd was the sole relative; Meridel pictured the entire Murphy family, wiped out, the men from leukemia and the women from living with them. Gradually their bodies had absorbed the ways of the dying. These thoughts frightened Meridel so she did not linger on them.

179

Two days after the funeral, Boyd drove off without explanation. And why should she expect anything? Meridel wondered stubbornly, watching the Murphy's car lumber around the corner onto the highway. He was grief-stricken, though she had not seen him cry. Still, she felt hurt, even betrayed. For days she felt this way and was miserable, missing him and Kyle and Mrs. Murphy banging pans, until it was all twisted inside and she wasn't sure who or what she was missing. On the third night he returned, flustered and gaunt but otherwise the same, and this knot of feelings passed. After he'd unpacked he came over and, instead of sitting on the porch, Meridel invited him into the kitchen for some freshly-baked bread.

"She was a frightened woman," he said. "She wasn't as gruff as people thought. She'd tiptoe around me, watching and waiting, making sure I did everything just right. She wanted things to be just so—in place—in case I died in my sleep."

Meridel thought of Mrs. Murphy's throat and the pans and the way she'd sat out in the car that night, one of her last, and Meridel urgently wanted to understand something that was just beyond her. She pulled at the bread, digging for the warmth, liking the feel of it in her fingers, the way the heat exploded in her mouth. "I suppose, as a mother, it was hard not to have those urges," Meridel said.

"But things can only be so in place, really, otherwise you learn nothing from the dying. Right? It would be pointless. If you're going to die, shouldn't you at least get something out of it?" He paused for breath, almost panting, brow wrinkled so the top half of his face looked older and more earnest than the lower. "Besides, in place is different from prepared. She spent so much time keeping things in place for my death, she wasn't prepared for the possibility of her own."

180

"But there was no reason for her to be, really. She was probably not even thinking about herself, knowing your condition."

Boyd pondered this, then nodded. Meridel was a little surprised with herself. Possibly, she thought, she just about had it right this time.

They talked in this manner night after night, until it was September, when one night they stayed up very late and Boyd did not return to his place. Instead he slept curled on her sofa, a dark humble shape, arms holding himself like someone missing a lover.

By morning they knew things had changed between them, and the following afternoon, when she returned from work, Boyd had moved a few things into her house. Nothing too obtrusive, just a few clothes and books and his pills and miscellaneous essentials—toothbrush, washrag, shaving kit. All these he kept in boxes pushed into every corner of the living room, except for the pills and personals, which he kept in the bathroom. They did not question or discuss this move. They seemed beyond that, somehow. They were following some higher order of things. Meridel did not know what this order was, precisely, but she did know that Boyd staying with her made perfect sense.

Boyd mowed her lawn, trimmed her hedges, pruned, dug, watered, and when he was through, he would go to his mother's yard and garden there. Then he began cleaning the inside of Meridel's house. He worked feverishly, pushing himself, a man with a deadline. "Between these two places, I could always be upkeeping," he said once, reeking of cleanser. "It would never end. There are so many things to fix, I could go on and on. It's a job without natural limits."

These days, after work, Meridel returned to a house that was never precisely the same as when she'd left it. Tiny changes were continuous, though at times she had to look hard to find them. Next door, the Murphy's place improved as well. This seemed sad to Meridel—its improvement was coming after it had been abandoned, with no one around to appreciate it. But she had gained from its loss, so she couldn't feel badly about the house for long.

They lived in this quiet watchful way well into October, when one night she heard Boyd moaning in his sleep. It wasn't from pain, this moaning, she thought; it was from the confusion caused by dreams. She listened. Now he seemed to be whispering. She listened harder, feeling mild guilt, but he went unexpectedly quiet. In the morning she meant to ask him how he was feeling, but his eyes carried a glazed far-off look and she felt oddly intrusive. So with difficulty, she let it go.

The next night she heard him moving in the living room, picking things up and setting them down again. She imagined him half-asleep and lost, a wraith searching through a land-scape he could not remember, trying to find the one object that would tell him where he was. She might have gone to him, but instead did not. She was afraid of what all this meant.

Then she heard a glass breaking and this filled her with a dread beyond what she could immediately place. She ran out to Boyd holding the sink with both hands and trembling. "I felt something move inside me," he said, his head bowed. "It felt like something was passing through me, then I went cold. I remember my father and mother fighting, once. I spilled my milk and my father yelled at me. So my mother yelled at him because he'd yelled at me and they put me outside in the yard while they argued. When they were through my mother let me inside and slapped my hands for making a mess. Why would I remember this now?"

Meridel touched the back of Boyd's neck. It was as though

182

she'd been dreaming of doing this, only to wake and discover she actually was. His was a warm neck, delicate, yet beneath the skin she felt the pull of tendons, of unseen muscles and veins. She couldn't do more than rub his neck, though. Their relationship wasn't like that. It was in another place, apart from physical yearning.

"I think, over the weeks, I've become more and more prepared for what's going to happen," he said, "but each day feel less and less ready. Do you see what I mean?"

Again Meridel wasn't sure, but she smiled anyway and lowered her hand to pick up the broken glass. She was trying to remember the last time she'd drunk from or held it. She could not remember. It had not been one of her favorite glasses, and it had not been an aggravating or chipped glass—it had been just a glass, serviceable, one of many.

"I have something to confess," he said, staring into a new glass he'd lifted to hold in his hand. "I confess I haven't been completely honest with you."

The urgency in his voice frightened her. Something was happening to them without her knowledge or understanding and she continued picking up the glass, not looking up.

"I confess that over the past week, I haven't been feeling like myself," he continued. "Something in me has changed. I knew that much. I could feel it. I thought the end must be coming near. The way I was feeling, what else could it be? That's what I couldn't tell you after all. That the end was coming. I know I promised I would but I didn't and couldn't. I waited until you were at work and then I went to the hospital to get the confirmation."

Boyd lowered the glass. Meridel pictured her life once he was gone. She could not bring it to mind. There was no picture for this. Boyd turned to her. She did not recognize the shirt he

183

was wearing.

"I've gone into remission," he whispered.

Meridel nodded but couldn't speak. Even after he repeated the phrase, twice more, softly, she still said nothing. Remission? It was as though she had never heard the word before.

"I couldn't tell you this either," he said. "I don't know why. I didn't know what to do with it myself."

Somehow she was no longer kneeling but sitting on the floor, now picking up the smallest glass shards and holding them in her hand. "Boyd," she said, but he'd wandered into the living room. She remained on the floor for some time, still holding glass chips in her hand, and when she stood, she still didn't know how to feel. Finally she understood she should go to him. He was lying on the sofa, one arm slung over his face. His shirt was off and she saw his chest, rising up and falling back. "It's wonderful news Boyd," she said. "You should be happy. We should both be feeling this more."

Boyd lowered his arm. His eye lashes glimmered, though he was not crying. "But everything's different now," he said. "That's what I'm feeling. I learned how to live with the idea of dying. Now the tables have been turned and I got all this life staring me in the face. You don't know the kind of feeling that is."

Though of course she did know. Kyle was not coming back, she could see that clearly now. He'd left her without much difficulty and possibly had no intention of returning all along. The two constants in Boyd's life—his mother and his death—were gone now too, and there Meridel and Boyd were, alone together, unsure of how to get on with things. The feeling was of betrayal.

"I think I should sleep now," he said. "Meridel? Do you understand? I got to sleep on this. I feel more tired now than I ever did when I was dying."

"Yes," she said. "Yes, that's right."

She drifted back into the kitchen, unfocused, dissatisfied. She was still holding glass in her hand and dumped this into the garbage. She had been very careful holding it, the whole time, but when she looked down at her palm, a tiny drop of blood swelled. She picked up the sink sponge and blotted it away. Outside there was not a sound. Not one. The world had sealed in on itself. Her head ached. The feeling was betrayal, yes, but a betrayal that ended in opportunity. There was more to it, she was sure, but she couldn't get at it.

She snapped off the kitchen light and started back to bed, but she stopped at the sofa, nearly against her will. She was aware that her hands trembled. Boyd was there, in front of her, and she felt farther from him now than she ever had during their nights waiting on the porch. Thinking there was an end had made things easy, she thought. Without it there were no guarantees and that was harder. Boyd was mumbling again, in what she imagined was an edgy, fierce sleep, but she couldn't hear what he said. She lay down beside him, still shaking, as though a living thing was trapped inside her, bucking to get out. She wrapped her arms around his chest, pressed her hands to where his heart pounded. His body tensed but he did not wake or pull away. As if she had planned it all along, she leaned over him and rested her ear close to his mouth. She wanted to hear what he was saying. Boyd's abandonment would end with a longer life, but where would hers end? She leaned closer still, as if his whispers would tell her. This was what she wanted from Boyd, she thought, even more than love or companionship. She wanted the words that would give her back her life.